The Journals of Major Peabody

A Portfolio of Deceptions, Improbable Stories and Commentaries about Upland Game Birds, Waterfowl, Dogs and Popular Delusions

by

Galen Winter

CCB Publishing
British Columbia, Canada

The Journals of Major Peabody: A Portfolio of Deceptions, Improbable Stories and Commentaries about Upland Game Birds, Waterfowl, Dogs and Popular Delusions

Copyright ©2010 by Galen Winter
ISBN-13   978-1-926918-06-8
First Edition

Library and Archives Canada Cataloguing in Publication
Winter, Galen, 1926-
The journals of Major Peabody : a portfolio of deceptions, improbable stories and commentaries about upland game birds, waterfowl, dogs and popular delusions / written by Galen Winter – 1ˢᵗ ed.
ISBN 978-1-926918-06-8
I. Title.
PS3573.I565J68 2010   813'.54   C2010-905786-4

The stories contained herein were first published in *Shooting Sportsman* magazine.

Publisher: CCB Publishing
              British Columbia, Canada
              www.ccbpublishing.com

For James Louis Larson

Contents

Major Nathaniel Peabody

The Peabody name has been present in the New World since the very beginnings of the Virginia colonization. The family has had a remarkable history - tobacco and cotton at first, then land, then investment banking and, always, philanthropy and public service. As is the case in all reputable families, occasional black sheep make their appearance. Major Nathaniel Peabody, USA, ret. is an excellent example.

The first entry in Major Peabody's list of life priorities is: Game bird hunting. Game bird hunting is also the second through (at least) the tenth item on that list. His life revolves around shotguns, dogs, hunting expeditions, hunting accessories and anything vaguely associated with bird hunting. All insignificant items - like food - are further down the list.

This explains why Major Peabody is incapable of managing money. It's not a good explanation, but it's the only one available.

For decades the prestigious Philadelphia law firm of Smythe, Hauser, Engels and Tauchen has represented the interests of the Peabody family. (I use the adjective "prestigious" because I am a junior member of the firm.) The Peabody Estate is substantial. I mean it is SUBSTANTIAL. Estate Planning is one of my law firm's areas of expertise and I was assigned the responsibility of drafting the Peabody Family Spendthrift Trust.

In the course of drafting that document, I had the opportunity to meet with the elder Peabody. He was well aware of his only son's frightful irresponsibility in matters financial. He gave me specific instructions designed to limit Nathaniel Peabody's ability to attack the corpus of the trust.

During his lifetime, Major Nathaniel Peabody would receive a generous monthly stipend, but (1) The amount of the remittance could not be increased, (2) The payment had to be delivered to the Major on the first day of the month, and not a moment earlier, (3) No prepayment of any kind would be allowed and, (4) No pledging or alienation of any remittance or segment of the trust corpus would be allowed.

I met Major Nathaniel Peabody in September of 1986 during the probate of the Jefferson Peabody Estate. It was not a pleasant meeting. The Major wanted a lump sum distribution of his inheritance. I could not allow it. He asked for a series of advance payments of his monthly installments. I could not allow it. I showed him the trust document, explaining its terms in detail.

Peabody was disappointed. He blamed me for his disappointment and, seeking revenge, I believe, he insisted on strict adherence to another portion of the trust provisions. As a result, I, as the Trustee of the Peabody Family Trust, must personally deliver his check at 12:01 a.m. on the first day of every month. Wherever the Major is at that time, I, too, must be there.

I am not a hunter. I'm not an outdoors man. I'm a city boy. Dogs don't like me. They bark at me. They snarl at me. I think they want to bite me. I'm afraid of all wild animals, like wolves or bears or porcupines or rabbits (many of them are rabid). I'm afraid of insects like wood ticks or mosquitoes or other crawling, biting things that carry terrible diseases. Nevertheless, on the first day of every month, when Peabody is usually in a tent or in a cabin in some uncivilized wilderness area, I must be there.

It hasn't been a bed of roses. However, it has not been without its pleasant moments. Through Peabody I met his hunting companion Doctor Carmichael. It's always nice to know a medical person who can determine if you have any of the new diseases the people on television discover and spend weeks warning us of the awful threat they represent. And it was the Major who introduced me to the lovely Stephanie.

Today I consider Peabody to be a good friend. Whenever the evening before the first of the month finds him in Philadelphia, we often dine together (at my expense because he is usually without funds). Later, we return to his apartment for night caps and conversations. I believe he considers me to be his friend, although, occasionally, I suspect he still blames me for the limitations on his ability to get his hands on the bulk of the Peabody estate.

Disappointment

I am convinced the senior partners of the Smythe, Hauser, Engels and Tauchen law firm decided to test my metal when they assigned me the task of managing the Peabody Spendthrift Trust. The trust instrument specifically requires remittances to be delivered on the first day of the month. That means I, personally, must deliver his check.

At the end of the month, Major Peabody is often "in the field". That means I often have to spend month-end evenings in backwoods cabins or tents, waiting for the stroke of midnight when I can hand Peabody his remittance and, as quickly as possible, return to civilization.

The first time I ever fired a gun was after the Major conned me into accompanying him on a Cuban duck hunt. Of course, I couldn't hit anything and when I returned, I had trouble with the Canadian Customs people. They accused me of smuggling because someone stuffed Cuban cigars down the barrels of my then new, but now confiscated Arrieta shotgun.

All my recollections of that trip are bathed in discomfort and distress. I remember the annoyance of not being able to appreciate the abusive camaraderie of the Major's hunting companions. I remember the irritation of being forced to eat black bean soup. I remember being terrified by the unprofessional looking system of bare and actively sparking electric wires running to the shower head and carrying current for the purpose of heating the shower water.

I remember the evenings listening to Major Peabody and

his friends as they talked about the various calamities they experienced during hunting expeditions. I most vividly remember the stories about encounters with ferocious animals and the deadly poisonous Cuban spiders and snakes and scorpions found in the immediate area of the rice field where we hunted. No one complained about those dangers. In fact, they all seemed cheerful about their misfortunes and perils - particularly if I seemed frightened by them.

I don't believe I'll ever understand hunters, but, then, I was born and raised in a Philadelphia suburb where golf and duplicate bridge were infinitely more respectable than shooting at things with shotguns.

* * * * *

I was in the Philadelphia airport, waiting to pick up Major Peabody and drive him to his apartment. The flight from St. Louis was on time. As Peabody came through the tunnel and into the waiting area, he cordially greeted me. We walked toward the luggage carousel and his conversation was light and infectiously jovial. Clearly, he was in a good mood.

"You must have had a good hunt," I observed. "How many turkeys did you kill?"

"Not one. I didn't even fire the gun." He smiled, apparently enjoying some private recollection. "I ran out of cigars and single malt," he said, still smiling, and showed only modest displeasure when reporting: "My host provided only blended Scotch."

Knowing Peabody's affection for imported cigars and aged single malt Scotch, the Missouri turkey hunt must have been a disaster. I wondered why he was in such good spirits. Then it came to me. "The Poker Gods smiled on you?" I asked. Peabody gave me a stern look supported by a pained expression. He answered my question with the statement: "I believe that's my luggage coming down the chute." I felt it prudent not to pursue the subject.

As we drove to his apartment, the Major avoided comment about the Missouri hunt. Still, his demeanor was that of a happy and satisfied man. Curiosity was killing me. After parking the car and bringing his baggage into his quarters, I could stand it no longer. "I'm sorry the turkey hunt was a disappointment." I expected the Major would describe the hunt and the disappointment and, thus, satisfy my curiosity.

Peabody was sitting in his wing backed chair next to the fireplace. "Disappointment? Disappointment?" he said, as if the thought never occurred to him. "I was in no way disappointed." He reached for the humidor containing his H. Upmann cigars. "I believe you'll find some of the Macallan under the sink," he said, casually. I took the hint and soon returned from the kitchen with a brace of Scotch and waters.

"Disappointment," he began, "is a product of improper expectation. 'Hope springs eternal from within the human breast' and when it is not fulfilled, hope ends in dis-appointment. A realist limits his expectations. Therefore, he limits his potential for disappointment. Hunters sometimes miss." He looked at the tip of his cigar, indicated satisfaction with the way it was burning and amended his statement.

"No. That's not right. Hunters often miss. They very often miss. Down deep, they don't really expect to hit what they shoot at. They are, thus, not disappointed when they miss, but they are elated when they happen to hit whatever they're shooting at.

"Duck hunters have learned to expect the worst. Even though the TV weathercaster has confidently promised a Saskatchewan Screamer bringing cold Canadian air, blustery winds and, probably, driving huge flight of late Bluebill before it, duck hunters go forth in pre-dawn November mornings expecting a day of calm, warm, bluebird weather.

"Turkey hunters, on the other hand, are always ready to experience the cold and the rain that keep them inside the cabin and the turkeys hunkered down, unmoving in the thickest of cover." (Now I know what happened in Missouri.) "Only the most naïve hunter expects a weatherman to tell the truth.

"Hunters know the elements and the fates conspire against him. The smarter ones avoid the disappointments by expecting their forays to end in disaster or, at best, discomfort. Thus insulated, misfortune brings no disappointment and their occasional successes bring them great satisfaction. That is the reason for the truism; 'All hunting trips are good. Some are better than others'.

"This does not mean the hunting fraternity sails through life without problems. I have been visited by bitter disappointment more than once. I embarked upon the sea of matrimony, expecting a calm and serene voyage. Soon buffeted by blackened skies, gale force winds and steep, angry swells, I suffered violent mal de mer.

"You may not believe this, but in my youth I harbored the insane expectation that the printed word was accurate. The particular text I have in mind appears on page 163 of the 1966 edition of The New Hunter's Encyclopedia. I still remember it: 'Experts claim that a skunk can be captured without danger of ejection if the tail is grasped and held down, possibly on the theory that the animal will not foul its own tail.' I vividly recall my extreme disappointment when I tested the theory.

"To avoid the destroyed hope which, surely, will result if you believe newspapers or any written publication, I suggest you begin by refusing to read the Congressional Record. Personally, I'm never surprised by those in political office. I expect so little of them there is no outrage they can commit that might cause me to be disappointed in them.

"But you, Counselor, live in a lawyer's world. You are constantly involved in planning to bamboozle judges, mislead juries, outwit tax collectors, and starve widows and orphans through manipulation of Spendthrift Trust provisions. What great expectations all of you must have. But, in every case, one lawyer wins and one lawyer loses. That means half the lawyers must be terribly disappointed when justice triumphs."

Peabody set his empty glass on the stand beside his chair and prepared to rise. "As I said, disappointment is the product of improper expectation. For example, during last night's unfortunate experience at the poker table, I was sustained by the knowledge that you fully expected to invite me to dinner. It is an entirely proper expectation and I won't disappoint you."

We went to Major Peabody's favorite restaurant.

Women's Rights

Never let it be said Major Nathaniel lacks proper respect for the female of the species. He neither derides their abilities nor considers them to be inferior to the male animal in any way. Frankly, I believe he is just a bit afraid of them. (Personally, I think men have good reason to be afraid of women.) His attitude may have been formed by the experiences he amassed during his short term marriage.

The Major's election never to re-marry supports my thesis. I believe he fears a wife might insist he become a better man and change what she would most probably consider to be his errant way of life It almost happened during his first venture into what turned out to be a very stormy relationship.

During the marriage, Peabody's Lefever 20 ga. gathered dust and complained of disuse. The Major was forced to start a savings account. In spite of the fact of his careful cleaning of the necklace after he retrieved it, his then wife insisted he get rid of his dog just because it had eaten that favorite bit of her jewelry. After the divorce Peabody felt like a slave who had been liberated. Undoubtedly, his ex felt the same way.

This does not mean the Major dislikes women. On the contrary, he enjoys their presence, but he has adopted the classic position enunciated by William Claude Dunkenfield who claimed: "A woman is like an elephant. I like to look at them but I wouldn't want to own one."

Major Peabody believes in the equality of the sexes. He treats women in the same way he treats his male associates.

This gets him into serious trouble with some members of the opposing sex, but others enjoy his fairness and his company. A case in point is the desirable and somewhat unattainable, lovely Stephanie.

The lovely Stephanie's family and the Peabody family have been friends for generations and she and I have been affianced for over five years. She is intelligent, independent and very committed to the causes of Women's Rights. It is her insistence on independence which has, I believe, delayed any formal ceremony legalizing our union. I'm sure she believes marriage amounts to some sort of surrender.

It was Major Peabody who was instrumental in first bringing us together. He had been invited to participate in a Western Hemisphere shotgunning expedition. It was to start with goose shooting in Greenland and then move south to Labrador for duck. The succeeding stops were: Upper Michigan for Ruffed Grouse, Iowa for pheasant, Mexico and Colombia for dove, Uruguay for Perdiz, Argentina for goose, and then back to Philadelphia for recuperation.

The mere thought of such an expedition was enough to cause Major Peabody to salivate. It was a once-in-a-lifetime hunt and he intended to participate. Of course, it was a very expensive undertaking. Of course, the Major had no backlog of funds available to support the costs of the five week project. When he asked for an advance from his Spendthrift Trust, of course, I had to again show him the terms of the Agreement which specifically allowed no advances of any sort.

Peabody reacted by contacting the lovely Stephanie for advice on how to convince me to allow advance payments of his monthly stipends. The lovely Stephanie and I met to confer prior to the initiation of legal action. The contractual limitations on Peabody's ability to get early distributions as well as the rights of the residual beneficiaries and my duty to protect the trust corpus were explained. I gave the lovely Stephanie a copy of the trust instrument.

After studying it, her attorneys concluded the document was carefully drafted and contained no loopholes through which Peabody could squeeze. The Major's attempt at legal action ended before it began. It also began my personal association with the lovely Stephanie. It has never ended (though, some of my friends believe it never really started.).

In spite of the (to him) disagreeable conclusion of his threatened lawsuit, Major Peabody, the lovely Stephanie and I remain good friends. Occasionally, the Major invites both of us to dinner at Bookbinders. Those invitations are usually extended during the last week of a month when Peabody is short of cash.

Privately, the lovely Stephanie tells me how much she appreciates the fact that Major Peabody does not insult her by adopting the male chauvinist insistence on grabbing the check. He allows her to pick up the bill. (In deference to maintaining my reputation with other customers who may be watching, the lovely Stephanie graciously allows me to pay the bill.)

The lovely Stephanie also appreciates the Major's sensitivity to other important issues of the Women's Rights movement. I've heard him tell her the women's tees at the golf courses should be destroyed since they suggest an inequality between the sexes. I've heard him tell her the popular trout fisherman's artificial fly should be re-named The Royal Coachperson. I've heard him tell her the Federal Department of Interior's Fish and Game people should be chastised for assigning 25 points to the drake Mallard and only fifteen to the hen.

If the lovely Stephanie has a minor flaw detracting from her perfection, it might be her strident attitude in regard to matters concerning women's rights and the equality of the sexes. Though the thought has occurred to me, I've never had the courage to suggest the Major might be putting her on.

I've certainly never hinted at my growing belief that men and women really are different. Women do strange things. They give peculiar anniversary gifts for one thing. I thought she knew I didn't hunt.

* * * * *

The Major crouched in a duck blind on a backwater of the Mississippi River near La Crosse, Wisconsin. He smiled as he thought of a dinner conversation with the lovely Stephanie.

In a few weeks, she had told him, it would be exactly five years since she and the Major's Trustee first met. Peabody took advantage of her comment to point out the traditionally established anniversary gifts were demeaning to women. The historically proper presents for an eighth anniversary (electric appliances), the ninth (pottery) and the thirteenth (lace) as well as the various gem stones were, in the Major's opinion, "based on the archaic attitude that the head of the household should give housewifely sops to the little woman".

Major Peabody went on to state: "This disparaging affront to women should be ended and assigned to the obscurity it deserves". Then, after mentioning the classic gift for the fifth anniversary was something made of wood, he said: "Stephanie, my dear, why don't you strike a blow for equality and instead of awaiting for some depreciating gift from your man, give him the anniversary present? And I know just the thing to give him."

The Major's reverie was broken when a flock of Bluebill, flying in their un-patterned and disorganized manner, came into sight. They responded to the Major's calling and came directly to his blind. They set their wings and slipped air as they dropped towards his newly acquired set of two dozen wooden decoys.

The decoys were a gift from the attorney who managed his Spendthrift Trust at the Smythe Hauser Engels & Tauchen law firm. (Major Peabody had to promise he would never tell the lovely Stephanie where or how he got them.)

The Education of a Grouse Hunter

On September 30, Major Peabody and I flew to Wisconsin. I accompanied him because I was obliged to personally deliver his trust remittance on the first day of October at 12:01 a.m. - the date when he would be in a deep woods cabin, awaiting sunrise and a day of hunting the Ruffed Grouse.

We went through customs in Milwaukee's Billy Mitchell Airport. After signing an affidavit swearing we brought no oleomargarine with us and denying we had ever been members of an organization dedicated to the overthrow of the cow or advocating the abolition of beer drinking, we were allowed to enter and Peabody bought an out-of-State hunting license.

The Major's three friends, dressed in their hunting togs, were waiting at the airport. They drove us to a backwoods cabin in the Central Wisconsin Conservation Area. The Major called it a cabin. I'd call it a shack. I was being charitable. It was only one small step above a hut.

On the following morning, I delivered the Major's check, but couldn't immediately return to Milwaukee for the flight to Philadelphia because "it was inconvenient". All of the men planned to hunt together on November 1. No one found it convenient to take me back to Milwaukee before the afternoon of the second day of November. As a result, I had to spend a day and a half in the Central Wisconsin woods. As a result, I felt an overpowering urge to "go hunting" with Peabody and his friends.

I am not a hunter. I'm afraid of guns and I'm afraid of

dogs. They enjoy barking at me and snarling at me and threatening me. Before the Wisconsin Ruffed Grouse trip, if you mentioned the term Bonasa Unbellus, I would have presumed you were talking about the head of a New Jersey crime syndicate. Nevertheless I wanted to spend the day hunting with Peabody and his friends.

If I didn't "go hunting", I would have to spend the entire day alone in the cabin, surrounded by wild animals. One look at that cabin convinced me snakes could easily crawl into it. They might have been in it at that very moment. I wondered if scorpions came that far north. I knew any sized black bear could easily knock the door down with one blow of its huge, razor sharp, clawed paws. When I heard the ominous sounds of distant drums, I decided I would be safer if I were surrounded by armed men. Hence my decision to "go hunting".

One of the men offered to let me use his back-up shotgun. I didn't want to touch the thing and tried to refuse it on the grounds of not having a Wisconsin hunting license. The host claimed it was all right. He hadn't seen a game warden in the vicinity for over ten years. Peabody said it was all right because I could afford to pay the fine and buy a replacement shotgun if one was confiscated. My objection was overruled.

My first day of hunting was an educational experience. I learned about grouse and grouse hunting and grouse hunters. Peabody's hunting companions consisted of a dentist, a publisher and a lawyer. (I understand it is usually necessary for grouse hunters to bring their own attorney with them.)

These men were my professors. I learned the scientific name for the Ruffed Grouse was Bonasa Umbellus. I learned the male grouse attracts the female by drumming his wings against his chest. That explained the drumming sound I had heard and I was relieved to learn the bird seldom attacks a human being.

That evening, in a poker game celebrating the coming hunt and substantially adding to the expenses of my trip, I learned grouse hunters are probably scoundrels and have to be watched when they deal the cards. I believe they were all trying to distract me from my game when they told me things like - on average, the grouse has 4,400 feathers - if you don't count the down.

Peabody describing the theories of the hunt. The dentist, nicknamed "Old Bang, Damn, Bang, Damn", the Major told me, ascribed to the "shoot and shoot and never aim" philosophy. The publisher (they called him "Slow Motion") had the reputation of swinging his gun barrel along a bird's line of flight until it was far beyond gun range. He was an adherent of the "aim and aim and never shoot" philosophy.

During the next day's hunt, my instruction continued. Finding me walking at the end of the line of hunters, the Major taught me to walk between the two men who owned hunting dogs. He explained it by saying the dogs will hunt in front of their owners and you'll get more action than will any idiot who hunts at the end of the line

I learned about grouse. If undisturbed by a hunting dog, they are capable of sitting as quietly as the guest of honor at a funeral. You can walk up to them or even past them before they flush. When one unexpectedly exploded from the underbrush beneath my feet, I learned to drop my gun, fall to the ground in alarm and panic and throw my arms over my head in a protective fashion.

The first time one of them erupted from beneath me. I found myself imploring Jehovah to please save me and promising, in exchange, to attend church every Sunday for a year. Five minutes later, when my heart rate was still a bit elevated and my palms still a bit moist, the bribe offered to Jehovah was reconstituted to provide for church attendance every other Sunday for six months.

I also learned how to carry a shotgun in grouse covert. While the "port arms" position is favored by many hunters, I like the less popular "cross arm" carry. With the gun cradled in the crook of my arm, at the sound of an exploding grouse, I was able to jump and turn in mid-air without dropping the shotgun more than half the time.

However, it was the "shoulder carry" that produced my success. With my right hand on the breech mechanism, I swung the two barrels of the shotgun up and backwards until they rested on my shoulder. At that moment, a bird flushed from right behind me and I panicked. I clenched my fist and inadvertently knocked off the safety. As I covered my head and reverently shouted out the name of deity, I squeezed the trigger and the gun went off.

I was surprised when the dog named Pfizer (a Lab, of course) ran back past me, found the unfortunate bird, returned and executed a perfect hand retrieve - to Major Peabody. Since the other members of the party knew he hadn't fired, he graciously handed the grouse to me and said "Nice shot".

I was proud of that Ruffed Grouse. Later, upon closer examination, I found it contained 4893 feathers - not counting the down. This was more than ten percent over the average for the species and, thus, a trophy specimen. I decided to have it mounted, but, after many hours of tedious work, I was able to replace no more than 2000 of the feathers. The bird was beginning to smell and I abandoned the project.

Where is Thy Sting

Major Nathaniel Peabody is the sole beneficiary of the Peabody Family Spendthrift Trust. It was established to insure him of a comfortable life. Major Peabody and the trust instrument have different definitions of the term "comfortable life". The Major thinks it means "whatever he thinks he needs". The trust document, however, clearly defines the amount of his monthly stipend.

Unable to negotiate an increase in the amount of his first-day-of-the-month remittances the Major has been forced to compromise. He lives quite frugally - if you don't count aged single malt Scotch whisky, imported cigars and every conceivable expenditure vaguely associated with shotguns, hunting equipment or hunting expeditions.

Some of Peabody's expeditions take him to exotic places in Europe or Africa or Latin America and are quite expensive. Others are more informal and less costly. Where Peabody hunts depends entirely upon the amount of cash contained in the cigar box he hides under his bed. Last month, the cigar box was nearly depleted. Peabody wanted to go to Maine. He came to me and explained the reason for his trip.

Unruly gangs were taking over large tracts of land in the northern part of that State. Behaving in a generally riotous manner, they violated the rights of the local inhabitants by disregarding No Trespassing signs and adversely possessing some of their properties. The Sheriff flatly refused to act on any of the complaints registered with him. He contended he had no jurisdiction because woodcock are considered to be migratory waterfowl and, as such, the problem was one for the federal government. Everyone knew it was an excuse. The sheriff was afraid of them.

According to Peabody, a friend, Jim Zimmerman, owned a cabin and a few forties in that part of the State. It was October and Zimmerman's property was infested with migrating woodcock. Outraged by their presence and desperate for relief, the man decided to take the law into his own hands. He bought a shotgun and a case of 7 ½ chilled shells and prepared to defend his property.

Days later, though his upper arm was black and blue, Zimmerman had failed to reduce the woodcock population. (Afterwards, he claimed he had only been trying to frighten them.) Zimmerman called Major Peabody and Doctor Carmichael, begging them to join him and a few friends and rid his property of those damned birds.

With this lengthy explanation and an appeal to "my well-known charitable impulse to help a fellow human being in dire straits", Peabody asked for an additional piece of the trust corpus in order to make his trip "more comfortable". It wasn't the end of the month. I refused his request and gave him a lecture on the need to more carefully control his expenses. Peabody had to undertake his expedition with no help from the trust monies.

* * * * *

The following day, Peabody and Carmichael met with the group convened at Jim Zimmerman's cabin. They formed a Vigilante Committee and sworn to maintain the peace, be kind to widows and orphans and drive the woodcock from the County. Peabody's initial impressions of the Committeemen were, by and large, favorable.

Their shotguns and hunting clothing did not have an unused look and one of the men brought dosages of top quality medicinal single malt Scotch to be used in the stead of the blended stuff provided by the camp. After paying for his air transportation, the Major's delicate financial condition did not allow him to provide for his own refreshments. His liquid funds were insufficient.

One of the Committeemen, however, did not pass muster. He was the camp cook. The Major had not seen a more disgusting, shifty-eyed and untrustworthy looking specimen since he visited the United States Senate. (This assessment of the man was confirmed when the cook admitted he was a banker from Milwaukee.)

The next day's hunt was successful. The Vigilantes had reason to believe - once their presence was more widely known - the hated woodcock would abandon the area with fear and trembling and decide to quickly migrate south, leaving the good people of Maine in peace.

After another good day in the field, when the hunters returned to the cabin, the Major's opinion of the cook proved to be correct. The man was unreliable. He neglected to bring a supply of soda crackers and milk for the pre-dinner hors d'oeuvres. His lack of planning forced him to provide sub-stitutions. Without consulting the other hunters, he prepared smoked oysters, ground round steak with onions and pepper on dark rye bread, aged cheddar cheese, and a clam dip with whitefish roe.

Peabody did not bring the man's failing to the attention of the others. The hunters were all good sports and used to adversity. They accepted the substitutes without complaint and proceeded to relax and review the day activities. By the time they were called to the dinner table, the sun was down, the kerosene lanterns were lit and the Major was telling a story about a gun with a crooked barrel and a constipated owl.

Perhaps it was the dim light - or the beverage - or the distraction caused by the stories. Major Peabody had not paid attention to what was going on about him. He had the fork inside his mouth before anyone was able to shout a warning.

The cook had soaked a dozen dead woodcock breasts in a marinade. Then he put them inside the woodstove oven. They lay there in that terrible heat for almost two hours before he took them out. Then, without warning or notice any kind, he served them to the entire company - just as if woodcock were edible.

Peabody doesn't like the taste of woodcock. No, that isn't right. Peabody detests the taste of woodcock. He has often warned me to turn and run if anyone suggests I take even the tiniest taste of one. He has assured me the flavor of the bird is improved by soaking it in kerosene for five days and then throwing it away.

Thought Peabody spit the disgusting woodcock onto his plate without swallowing, the taste lingered in his mouth and in his memory. It had been a very close call. I'm sure it was this brush with catastrophe that caused Peabody to consider his own mortality and begin to "make provisions".

As soon as he returned from Maine, he called on Peter Klemmens to take care of his mortal remains. Peter Klemmens is not a funeral director. He is a taxidermist. Peabody was impressed by his work when he saw a deer head mount Peter had done over twelve years ago. Not one hair had fallen out. "When the time comes", Peter has agreed to stuff the Major for eight dollars an inch.

Peabody felt he had done a good job in negotiating the price. He proudly told me how he was changing his ways and watching his non-hunting expenses.

Providence

Major Nathaniel Peabody and two companions were in a hunting lodge in northwestern Uruguay. They came to hunt the Perdiz runing in the fields surrounding Hector Sarasola's hunting lodge and the Gray Spotted Pigeons clouding the skies above it. The lodge's ads assured the hunters they could fire at least two cases of shells per day. Hector confirmed that promise and assured them they would arrive in Uruguay during the most productive part of the season.

This was not the first time Peabody hunted with the other men. They became acquainted in a field full of pheasants in South Dakota. A second meeting took place in a Minnesota grouse camp. This would be their third reunion.

A small chartered plane carried them from the airport at Montevideo to the city of Mercedes where a waiting truck delivered them to Sarasola's Lodge and their countryside hunting grounds. After promising to re-convene for a pre-dinner period of libation and relaxation, the men went directly to their assigned quarters. The outlook for the three day hunt was most promising.

As Major Peabody unpacked his gear, he reviewed the results of his most recent poker game. It occurred the evening before he left Philadelphia for this hunt. Those results were not entirely satisfactory. Those results were in no way satisfactory. The results were terrible. Peabody had been nearly wiped out.

It was the twenty-fifth day of the month. The Major would be back in Philadelphia one day before the end of the month when his grossly inadequate supply of money would be replenished. In the meantime, however, the Major had to have enough cash to buy shotgun shells, pay for personal expenses and give his Uruguayan guide and the Lodge staff their expected tips.

Even if Peabody limited his shooting and exercised unaccustomed good judgment with regard to non-essential spending, he would still fall far short of the amount he needed. His tiny supply of cash could not be stretched to cover even his absolute minimum projected expenses. "Well," he said aloud, "I wonder if I could get a bit of help from my friends." Those prospects were dim, indeed.

Sandy Hausman owned an automobile dealership. Sandy did not have sandy hair. As his surname indicates, he was not a Scot. He was a German. He was not a blond Nordic. He was the black haired, Baltic kind of German. He got the nickname "Sandy" because of his super-frugal nature. The most conservative, close-fisted Scotsman would admire him.

Sandy Hausman was a stingy man. He was often described as "tighter than the bark on a paper birch tree". He was very good at accumulating money, but an abject failure when it came to disbursing it - any of it. For example, while the three hunters were enjoying libations during their four hour stop-over in Miami, not once did Sandy's hand find his wallet.

Nevertheless, Major Peabody admired Sandy. He and Sandy once came out of a Minnesota woods and found themselves on a dirt road close to a country tavern. Smelling a bit un-bathed and with a beard grown during a four day Ruffed Grouse hunt, Sandy convinced the bartender he was a man of the cloth and, thus, entitled to what he called "the usual clergyman's fifteen percent discount on drinks". You have to admire a man who can do that.

Admirable or not, Sandy Hausman's record of making

loans was perilously close to being completely non-existent. He was known to occasionally - very occasionally - engage in wagering, but only when the potential for loss was minimal. Actually, less than minimal - infinitesimal would be a better description. (And, if possible, less than infinitesimal.) To attempt to pry money from Sandy Hausman was a heroic, Herculean labor.

The other hunter, Steve Gress, was a successful personal injury attorney. Successful personal injury attorneys are experts at scaring the living bejaysus out of casualty insurance companies and doing enormous damage to the reserves established for claim payment. Steve Gress was an expert con artist. He knew all the tricks of deception because he practiced every one of them.

The Major appreciated Gress's ability to mislead and defraud - characteristics common to all good damage attorneys. He knew the lawyer was very careful when it came to betting. Steve would be a man difficult to outsmart.

When it came to wagering, Peabody, the used car salesman and the personal injury attorney were three of a kind. Each one was cautious. Each one was schooled in duplicity. Each one always assumed his associates had something up their sleeves. Each one was hard to fool. The Major knew he would not have an easy time of it.

Peabody sighed and resigned himself to a week of austerity and, perhaps, some unpleasantness when it came time to pay the bill. "We live in an imperfect world," he said to himself as he unpacked his gear. He left the room and began to walk to the lodge patio just as Sandy Hausman came into the hallway from the adjoining room.

"How goes it, Major?" he asked, "Ready for tomorrow's hunt?

"Ah, Sandy, my boy," the Major answered, trying to find a

palatable explanation for his lack of funds. "I'm afraid misfortune has visited me."

"Nothing serious, I hope."

"Oh, no. Nothing serious - merely a temporary inconvenience." The explanation came to him. "All that jostling and crowding in the airport at Montevideo. I'm afraid someone picked my pocket. He got my wallet, credit cards and all." Peabody hoped Hausman might offer temporary relief from his predicament. It was a forlorn hope. Sandy limited himself to saying "A pity, Major. A pity. You have my sympathy." (Sandy was known for his generous offerings of sympathy to those in financial distress.)

The Major and Sandy sat at a table on the patio and awaited the arrival of Steve Gress. Hausman ordered a drink - for himself. Then a thought occurred to him. He leaned forward in his chair. "Major," he said. "I may be able to help you out. Suppose I were to advance the price of, say, four cases of shell. Suppose I were to bet Steve I'd get more birds that you. What would you think of that?"

Major Peabody had a number of thoughts. One of them was: Providence was smiling upon him.

"Two things occur to me, Sandy," he answered. "The first is: What's in it for me? I noticed you used the word 'advanced'. Second: I presume you intend to somehow take advantage of our attorney friend. Correct?" Sandy nodded. "Well, then," Peabody continued, "if you bet Steve you'll take more birds than I will, Steve will wonder why you haven't bet with me. He'll know something is up. We'll have to be more subtle."

Sandy puzzled over the problem. He wanted to tap Steve, but the thought of actually paying for the Major's shells was dreadful. The Major watched Sandy struggle with the dilemma before coming to his rescue.

"Suppose," Peabody suggested, "you were to give me six cases of shells." The word 'give' was emphasized. "Suppose you were to bet me a thousand dollars you'd get more birds than I would. Suppose - just between ourselves - we agreed any debt that might be owed as a result of our bet would automatically be cancelled. What would you think of that?"

Sandy looked shocked. "I think I'd be crazy to accept that one. I'd be sure to lose the price of six cases of shells."

"Don't be too hasty, Sandy," Peabody said. "Let me explain. Steve is cagey. If he hears me take your thousand dollar bet, I think he'll bet another thousand I'll outshoot you. If he bets with you, you could win a thousand from him. What's a case of shells worth down here? Ten bucks a box? Six cases? That's six hundred dollars. You'll make four hundred, net, if he bites."

Sandy smiled. It sounded good to him, but he wanted to make sure. "How much money do you have?" he asked.

Peabody admitted to having thirty-two dollars and sixty-three cents.

"That's it?" Sandy asked.

"Yup."

"If Steve doesn't bite, we cancel our bet and you owe me for the shells. Right?

"Right."

"If Steve does make the thousand dollar bet, we cancel the shell debt and our own thousand dollar bet. Right?"

"Right'"

In order to make his proposition "suitable", Sandy proposed some additional agreements. "First, we agree to reduce my investment from 6 to 4 cases of shell and you agree to shoot them all in the first two days. Right?"

"Right."

Sandy's final condition was: "You agree you won't shoot

more birds than I do during those first two days. Right?"

"Right."

They shook hands. Peabody was pleased. At the very least, he got Sandy Hausman to provide four cases of shotgun shells. He might have to re-pay Sandy for the shells, but he'd gone a long way toward solving his cash flow problem.

Sandy was also pleased. He wouldn't lose a cent if Gress didn't bet. Peabody would have to pay for the shells. If Steve bet, Peabody would not outshoot him during the first two days and Peabody would be out of shells and with no money to buy them for the last day of the hunt. Sandy couldn't lose. When Steve came to the patio, they were ready for him. They watched until he got close to the table - close enough to hear the Major say: "You've got a bet, Sandy."

"What kind of a bet?" Steve asked and he learned Sandy bet a thousand dollars he'd drop more birds than the Major during their three day hunt. Steve had seen them both in action. He knew Major Peabody could outshoot Sandy any day of the week. Sandy was clever about it. He acted as if he was a bit reluctant to agree to Steve's thousand dollar bet on Peabody.

At the end of the second day, the Major did well with the Perdiz, but fired injudiciously at the pigeons. He managed to shoot two birds fewer than Sandy Hausman. Peabody was out of shells and Sandy Hausman was happy.

* * * * *

During the flight back to Miami, it was Sandy's time to be unhappy and Steve was gloating. At the end of the second day, while they waited on the patio for Sandy to join them, Peabody told Steve he was out of shells and out of money. Steve offered to give him two more cases for the next day's shoot. The Major agreed to accept the shells, but only if Steve paid the tips owed to his guide and the lodge

Sweet Charity

It was one o'clock in the morning. The Coleman lantern shone through the window, giving a bit of outside light to a raccoon busily scattering the content of the garbage bag left next to the kitchen door. Inside the cabin, two men slouched in their chairs. A third had his elbows on the poker table and his head in his hands. They appeared to be dispirited and quietly contemplating some painful experience. The fourth man, Major Nathaniel Peabody was smiling and stacking the chips piled up before him.

"Gentlemen," he said as he rattled the ice cubes in his empty glass, "Look upon it as a learning experience. When you compare the instruction you've received tonight with the costs of university tuitions, the lessons have been quite inexpensive."

The silent hunters regained their voices. One of them snorted and complained: "The only thing I've learned is to avoid decks of cards that refuse to help me when I hold four card flushes".

The man at the ice chest, now refilling Peabody's glass, said: "The Poker Gods are the ones who failed to smile upon me. They're the ones who have done me in."

Without looking up, the hunter with his head in his hands muttered: "We should replace that Beware of the Dog sign with one that says "Beware of the Peabody".

The Major showed no reaction to the unkind statement. "For nearly a century," he explained, "psychiatrists have insisted personal responsibility no longer exists. They believe the ax murderer, who attempts to solve the world's over-population problem in his own special way, is not responsible for his acts. Blame, they tell us, should be assigned to someone else - usually the killer's parents who must have engaged in forcing him into potty training at too early an age.

"Ever since our prehistoric progenitor, Homo habilis, developed the opposing thumb and, thus, was able to shuffle a deck of cards, gambling losses have been blamed on bad luck. Shooting both barrels and missing every one of the ducks in the flock wheeling over your decoys has also consistently been blamed on bad luck.

"Yes," he continued, "when things go wrong, it is the well established and time honored practice to point the finger of blame at someone else. However, I must disagree with you. I believe you err in blaming your collective misfortune at the poker table on bad luck, on the perversity of a deck of cards, on the Poker Gods or, for reasons I am unable to comprehend, on me.

"Anthropologists believe the dinosaurs evolved into modern day birds. Think of it. It's truly an amazing feat. However, the genus Homo sapiens has accomplished an even more amazing achievement. It developed the concepts of Faith and Hope and Charity, the three most admirable qualities found in the human being. The facility to believe - to have faith, the ability to hope and the capacity to extend charity distinguishes mankind from the lower animals.

"It would appear the biblical pronouncement promoting Faith, Hope and Charity has not fallen on deaf ears. Tonight each of you has confidently confirmed your belief in those three admirable concepts. In spite of odds that would cause most men to muck their cards, you have displayed a surprising hope that the card needed to fill an inside straight or change two pairs into a full house would be dealt to you. Still, in spite of many disappointments, your faith in the delivery of the card has not wavered.

"I am particularly thankful for your faith and hope. Of course, it would be unkind of me not to mention my appreciation for the charity you have shown in following and, on occasion, raising my bets. I acknowledge my appreciation for the funding your faith, your hope and your charity have brought me. You have all been very kind."

Peabody paused while his audience snorted and groaned and someone asked: "Can't anybody shut him up?"

The Major allowed a faint smile to cross his face and continued. "I won't criticize your acceptance of faith, hope and charity because I must admit they, too, has been the rule and guide of my life. Only through the exercise of unbelievable self control have I been able to disregard them while seated at the poker table this evening. Most men could not disregard the driving urges I have felt to contribute to your welfare. However, my strength is as the strength of ten because my heart is pure"

Peabody's admission was duly acknowledged by his companions. Their comments were: "I think I'm going to throw up" and "Please stop. I'm allergic to bull by-product" and "Sanctimonious son of a female dog".

Peabody paid no attention to them. "This evening, my charitable urges have been overwhelming and I have nearly found myself deciding to give each of you twenty dollars. I've tried to convince myself such a gift would be an appropriate rebate for your kindness and generosity at the table. After the most careful of consideration, I have rejected the thought. I know you are all too proud to accept charity."

Murmurs of protest began and one of the three hunters stood and said: "I'm not" while another yelled out: "Just try me."

Peabody quickly held up his hand to quiet them. "No. No," he said. "I'm sure not one of you would stoop to accept an outright gift of a part of the money you had honorably lost at the gaming table. At the same time, the charitable urge within me is so strong I cannot deny it. You see my problem, don't you? I want to give and you are too proud to accept. Whatever shall I do?"

The Major thought for a moment and then cried out: "Eureka. I believe I have found a path around my dilemma. Suppose you were to make a bet with me. If you won, you would not be humiliated by receiving charity and my urge to soften your poker losses would be honorably satisfied. I would not have offered charity. You would not have accepted charity."

Peabody's statement was greeted with skepticism and distrust.

"Look out. He's got something up his sleeve."

"I wouldn't bet with Peabody if he was the last man on earth."

"I would bet with Peabody - but only if he was the last man on earth."

Major Peabody went to the ice chest, opened it and removed an orange. He placed it in the center of the poker table and slowly shook his head in disappointment. "So much for good deeds," he said. "Out of the generosity which is so characteristic of my being, I was going to bet each of you twenty dollars that I could tell the exact number of pips inside this orange."

Abrupt silence followed as the three hunters showed unmistakable signs of interest in the proposition. They huddled and softly analyzed the bet.

"Is it one of those seedless oranges?"

"No. The one I ate had lots of seeds."

"Do you think he opened that one and counted them?"

"You don't think he's telling the truth, do you?"

They looked at each other and found agreement.

"You've got a bet," one of them said, "but we get to select the orange. OK?"

Major Peabody nodded his agreement. With a smile of Christian charity, he began to peel the substituted orange. "I'll tell you the number of pips," he said, "just as soon as I open this thing and count them."

His fellow hunters screamed imprecations and called him a cheat, a swindler, and an unmitigated scoundrel. Peabody calmly denied their accusations. "I am, in fact, a true devotee of sweet charity," he protested and then added, "As you all know, charity begins at home."

Rain

The shack covered an area no larger than eight feet by sixteen feet. It was located between a forested plot and twenty acres of incompletely harvested corn. If there had been a finished ceiling, the room would have been seven feet high. The structure housed a broken bunk, a table, chairs and a wood stove made out of a fifty-five gallon oil drum. Major Peabody said he thought the roof had to be older than the building. It allowed a number of leaks. One of them dripped directly onto the stove. The water sizzled when it landed on it.

A window graced the south wall. Three of its panes were glass. The other was a piece of weathered corrugated paper. The door had seen better days. Binder twine was threaded through the hole where the door knob should have been. The other end of the twine was tied to a bent nail driven into what was left of the door jam. It nearly held the door shut. No one knew when the place had been abandoned, but it wasn't a recent occurrence.

In addition to the Major, the shack also contained three other hunters and two dogs. They were all very happy to be there. It was raining outside. Not drizzling. Heavily raining. Had it been drizzling, the men would have been in the field, watching their dogs enthusiastically wagging tails and snuffling the ground in search of pheasants. Now, the dogs sat with their muzzles on their owner's laps, getting their ears scratched and filling the small room with the special perfume coming only from wet dog hair.

When four hunters and three dogs are crammed into a small shack, they'll talk about hunting. (The dogs won't talk. They'll sit, get their ears scratched and listen in the often disappointed hope of learning something intelligent.) As surely as the night follows the day, the men will recount their own experiences.

Major Peabody slid a shingle into a slivered rafter in order to funnel the drips away from the stove and Tom Rosenow took the floor.

"Jim. Do you remember the time we were hunting grouse up near Watersmeet?"

"Yes, I remember it." Jim couldn't forget it. Tom wouldn't let him. Every time they met he was sure to tell the same story. Each time the story was embellished a bit more until neither of them recalled exactly what had happened.

"Your dog. Sparkle, chased up a bird and it flew off to my right, dodging around the popple trees. It was a long and difficult shot - I'd say about fifty yards - but I tried it anyway. The bird took a ninety degree turn, flew through some balsams and disappeared into a swamp. You remember, Jim?"

"I remember," Jim said quietly. He knew what was coming.

"Well, Jim came over and took great delight in giving me a three minute lecture on wasting shells, shooting at out-of-range birds and, by missing, disappointing his dog. Just as he was getting into a full barrage of abuse, Sparkle came out of the swamp with the grouse in its mouth. I'll never forget it."

"You'll never let me forget it," Jim muttered. He could have told an entirely different version of Tom's story, but would have run a serious risk of violating the Hunter's Code of Ethics. Shotgun hunters tend to be polite fellows. They allow the story teller some leeway with regard to absolute truth. They expect a certain amount of poetic license and will accept the accuracy of a fellow hunter's story even if such acceptance requires a super active imagination.

"It doesn't take much to knock down a Ruffed Grouse," Jim said. He was anxious to change the subject. He knew Tom was about to embark on an extended declaration of his justifiable pride and recognized accuracy in the firing of shotguns.

"A single 7½ chilled BB will do the trick. Sometimes they'll fly after being hit. I remember one time I was hunting with Peabody in Forest County. The Major raised a bird. He shot and it flew away. We both thought he missed it. I walked for about another fifty feet and heard something in the branches above me. I looked up in time to see the Major's grouse drop out of the tree. It fell at my feet and it was dead, dead, dead. Isn't that right, Major?"

"Absolutely," Major Peabody lied. "I remember it just as if it were yesterday."

"I don't doubt it for a moment," Bruce Sim, the third hunter, confirmed, signaling he was about to tell some questionable tale and expect Jim, in turn, to back him up. "But, sometimes a single BB won't bring them down. I was hunting near the South Branch of the Oconto on opening day. Lots of birds around. I had a limit and was back in camp before noon. I didn't go out with the guys in the afternoon. I decided to give them a treat and cook some grouse for dinner.

"I made a Hollandaise sauce for the broccoli, baked some potatoes, chilled a few bottles of Liebfraumilch and then went to work on the grouse. The meal was delicious. Everyone was in a pleasant mood and things were going well until Doc Carmichael bit down on a BB and broke a tooth. Then things got exciting. There were threats of lawsuits and million dollar damage claims for pain and suffering. There was talk about avoiding the lawsuit by shooting Doc Carmichael and leaving his body in the woods for the Ravens.

"I wasn't the least bit worried. When things began to get

out of hand, I reminded them I was not the kind of person who would ruin meat. I always shoot grouse in the head. The men were quickly convinced the grouse in question must have been shot during the previous season. It carried the BB inside it for an entire year."

The three other hunters sat silently considering the story. After a few moments they nodded, agreeing the story was probably accurate. Then everyone looked to the Major. It was his turn. Peabody surveyed his companions and began by quoting Shakespeare.

"Hamlet said: 'There are more things in heaven and earth than are dreamt of in your philosophy.' There are more exceptional events involving the Ruffed Grouse than the uninitiated can conceive. Still, those exceptional events do occur. Some years ago, the Michigan Ruffed Grouse Season opened on the day after the close of the Trout Season. I got to John Schmid's cabin the day before hunting grouse was legal. A note informed me John was in town looking for supplies.

"The cabin was near the Tamarack River and John left his fly rod on the porch. To use up time, I picked up the rod and walked to the stream. I was back in the cabin when John returned. When I presented him with a Ruffed Grouse, John accused me of poaching. I suppose, technically, I may have fractured some Michigan Fish and Game Regulation, but, given the circumstances, I don't believe any U P jury would convict me.

"I explained what had happened. I told John I did not shoot the bird, but, can you believe it, he did not believe me. He thought I shot it or, perhaps, it committed suicide by flying into my car. I carefully skinned the bird. There were no bruises on the body. Neither were there any BB holes. The only mark was a deep gash on the bird's neck.

"Gentlemen, that bird flew across the Tamarack River just

as I was in the middle of a back cast. My fly hooked its neck and broke it."

Peabody stopped and looked at his friends. They were quiet. They wouldn't look him in the eye. To bolster his story, the Major added: "I was using a Hair Wing Adams on a three pound test leader." It didn't help. One by one the men got up and walked out into the heavy rain. The dogs, with heads down and tails between their legs, followed them.

The Future is Before Us

When the lovely Stephanie asked Major Peabody to attend one of her soirees, he said he'd be delighted to attend. He wouldn't be delighted to attend. Peabody detests those kinds of social event, but he likes the lovely Stephanie. In addition, the lovely Stephanie's invitation meant he could exchange his accustomed late-in-the-month breakfast, lunch and dinner diet of boxed macaroni and cheese for the goodies that would grace her hors d'oeuvre table.

Peabody knew the invitation also meant he would be expected to mingle with people who didn't hunt. Their knowledge of dogs was limited to the Pekinese, the Shi Tzu, and other small, hysterical, disgusting, ankle biting non-hunting breeds. He was willing to undergo the ordeals of conversation with those people only because he expected he would be able to dull his sensibilities with the aged single malt Scotch usually accompanying the lovely Stephanie's parties.

I provided the Major's transportation to and from the affair. From the moment we arrived, I knew Peabody's evening would not be easy. There was no single malt hidden among the bottles of red and white wine set out on the buffet.

There was, however, a plentitude of conversation covering a spectrum of subjects in which the Major had no interest whatsoever. His body language clearly signaled his tedium and his discomfort. I kept an eye on him, intending to quickly intervene in the event I saw signs of impending social disaster. In deference to the lovely Stephanie, the Major behaved himself fairly well. He made only two tiny missteps.

A tweedy birdwatcher approached Peabody and asked him to identify a visitor to her backyard feeder. She described it as having a yellow tail and catching flies. I don't believe she understood what the Major meant when, after thinking for a moment, with some authority he told her it was a Chinese Outfielder. She said it must be a rare species and she would look it up in her bird book.

When Peabody tried to enter a discussion about genetic engineering, I tried to save him from embarrassment by saying I, too, knew a Mr. Gene Splicing. However, the Major showed more than a casual interest in the conversation that followed. He became fascinated by the subject of DNA manipulation and genetic engineering.

Later, as I drove him back to his apartment, Peabody's enthusiasm was obvious. "We live in an amazing time, my boy," he bubbled. "For centuries scientists have wasted their time trying to transmute lesser metals into gold, attempting to send a man to Mars and torturing humanity by inventing the computer and the internet with its cookies and pop-ups. Now, for the first time in the memory of man, they appear to be performing a valuable service for the human race.

"Just think of it. They are able to sneak into the DNA helix, grab the bits that produce undesirable characteristics and then replace them with ones that will correct Mother Nature's flagrant errors. Do you know what that means?" he asked. "Within our lifetime we will see grains engineered to grow in both the heat of the warmest climates and in the snows of the coldest winters."

"Yes, Major," I agreed. "It is truly amazing. After years of experiment, scientists can create seeds able to resist attacking disease. It is an accomplishment of enormous import not only for those who grow grains but also to those who consume them. Larger harvests and more food can eliminate starvation from the face of the earth."

"Yes. Yes, I suppose so," Peabody said, dismissing my observation. "I hadn't thought of that modest collateral advantage. I was concentration on the more important benefits." The Major raised his eyes and looked off into the future. "I see pheasants thriving in fields of corn growing in the hot Arizona desert. I see them surviving and growing fat on corn growing out of the winter snow on the frigid North Dakota/Canada border.

"I see hearty wild rice quickly reproducing to fill waterways. I see vigorous duck celery and duck potato plants designed to crowd out lily pad congestion and restore lakes and streams to vibrant waterfowl habitat. I see clouds of ducks flying into those excellent re-established feeding grounds, renewing pass shooters' faith in the existence of a Supreme Being.

"I see foxes engineered to eschew the eating of pheasants. I see them developing a diet consisting exclusively of rodents. I see future Pine Martens losing their interest in Ruffed Grouse and their eggs. I see them subsisting solely on the meat of dead porcupines.

"I see flocks of starlings descending upon the springtime fields and forests where they will eat huge volumes of wood ticks. I see wood ticks being listed on the official endangered species lists. I see the Sierra Club disintegrating over the internal struggle of whether or not they will expend their treasury to protect the tick. In short, my young barrister friend, I see a bright and shining future."

I'll admit I was a bit miffed by the Major's insensitivity to the problem of starvation.

"I don't share your confidence in the abilities of the scientific community," I told him. "A miscalculation in some university laboratory could result in the mutating of a virus, changing it from one that causes nothing more than the common sniffles into one becoming a primary cause of death. Some mad scientists could create a species of huge ravenous mosquito unaffected by Deet laden sprays and able to remove an man's entire blood supply with a single feeding."

"There," I said to myself, *"that ought to give him something to think about."* The Major, however, would not be dissuaded. "Pish and Tosh," he snorted. "Outdoorsmen have been fighting mosquitoes for centuries. Malaria and Yellow Fever couldn't stop us from producing the long list of achieve-ments we have given to mankind."

"Long list of achievements?" I asked myself. *"Whatever is he talking about?"* Peabody must have noticed my expression of surprise and disbelief. He merely looked at me and said: "For one thing, you wouldn't be enjoying steaks or pork chops it hunters hadn't weaned Homo erectus from a diet of roots and nuts and berries."

"Scientists might start out by splicing the DNA of grains," I countered, "but it wouldn't be long before they'd be playing around with Homo sapiens. Don't be too quick in your unconditioned support of genetic engineering, Major. Once the genetic genie is loose it will be impossible to control.

"Mary Shelly's tale of Doctor Frankenstein may be less of the fiction than we have heretofore imagined," I told him, "That good doctor's intentions may have been praiseworthy but, before you get too carried away, remember he produced a homicidal maniac. Lord knows what will happen when Doctor Frankenstein's modern day counterparts start fooling around with human DNA. Personally, I don't look forward to a race of people who have two heads or three arms."

"Don't dismiss human genetic engineering," Peabody continued. "The New World monkeys have prehensile tails.

Tails are handy things to have. They can act as a rudder when you swim. If bow hunters' DNA was programmed to give them tails, they could use them to hold onto branches when they were up in their trees stands. Fewer of them would be injured by falling out of the trees.

"A moment's thought will produce hundred of examples of good work the genetic scientist will be able to accomplish by tinkering with the human being. The world will be a much better place after they have identified and removed that part of the DNA chain producing the traits universally shared by used car salesmen, politicians, Trust attorneys and other con artist miscreants."

At that moment we arrived at the Major's apartment building and I was spared from what I was sure would be one of the Major's diatribes aimed at my profession.

Shorty's Story

Major Nathaniel Peabody is convinced the primary problem facing the nation is not represented by the threat of terrorists, by crooked bankers and stockbrokers, or by liberals and other felons. He contends it is the presence of insane contract provisions limiting a beneficiary's access to Spendthrift Trust funds.

A survey of the Major's hunting associates shows the majority of them believe the country's greatest danger is the United States Congress. Closely following are the large percentage of hunters who are convinced the most important question requiring the Republic's attention is: Which breed is the best bird hunting dog. Shorty Powell has struggled with that question for years.

Like many in the Upper Michigan, Shorty is an avid hunter, fisherman, out-of-doors-man and practitioner of what is locally known as The Powell Program. (The Powell Program consists of two stages. In the Spring, one pawns his deer rifle and buys trout and lake fishing equipment. In the Fall, one sells his fishing equipment and gets his deer rifle out of hock.)

Shorty is often among the unemployed. He is often unemployed because employment gets in the way of his more important endeavors. It's a matter of getting one's priorities in proper order. Who, Shorty asks, should go into the woods to cut pulp when the trout season is open? Who, he asks, should be expected to punch in at the saw mill time clock when the deer season is open? Can any rational human being avoid quitting and taking up a shotgun when Ruffed Grouse hunting is legal? Shorty's answers are: "No one", "No one," and "Of course, not."

When the government's Stimulus Package was first unveiled, Shorty was skeptical. He wondered if many of the proposed uses of taxpayer money were really necessary expenses - like the hundreds of thousand of dollars awarded to study tattoo removal in California, school bullying in Montana, grape genetics in New York and swine odor in Iowa. He doubted such spending was designed to bring the country out of recession. He harbored the strange suspicion the purpose of the Stimulus Package was to fund projects designed to pay off politicians' cronies.

Then Shorty had an epiphany. The government was about to spend a kazillion dollars. Even if one is silly enough to presume Congress has an interest in controlling and accounting for such spending, there is no way it can be done. Washington is embarking on a program of throwing basketfuls of money into the air. As it floats down to earth, anyone can run out into the street and grab some of it.

Shorty remembered an axiom his father told him: When the gravy train is rolling, get aboard. Why shouldn't at least some of that government money be used for a worthwhile purpose? Why not use it to study hunting dogs? Shorty Powell went to his friend, Major Nathaniel Peabody, for advice on how to proceed. The Major supported Shorty's idea and told him to contact his congressman.

Shorty was unable to speak directly with his House of Representatives politician. The only time the fellow ever left Washington D C to visit his Congressional District was when he was running for re-election and wanted his picture taken in a trout stream to show people he was a true outdoorsman and environmentalist. Many of his constituents had threatened his life. On the few occasions when he visited his District, the Congressman's bodyguards keep everyone far away from him. He was never within the range of their deer rifles.

Shorty wrote a nice letter to the fellow. He referred to tree grafting. It allowed people to retire in Florida and get oranges, grapefruit and lemons from the same tree. He recalled animal cross breeding producing bossy cows with more butter fat per square quart of milk and beef cattle with more protein per bale of hay. He pointed out the improvements in the science of horse breeding. It resulted in the construction of race tracks bringing hundreds of thousands of dollars into bookies' bank accounts.

With appropriate government stimulus funding, Shorty wrote, he would embark on a scientific study of cross-bred dogs. His study, he claimed, would produce similar long range benefits for mankind. Without further explanation, he asked for a thousand dollar grant and promised to use the grant to alleviate Upper Michigan's terrible unemployment problem and strengthen the local economy.

Shorty told the truth. If he got the grant, his project would give him a paying job. He would spend every cent of the grant for the supplies and other items essential to his investigations. Those essential items included: A supply of Dago Red, a dog, a dog collar, a bell, dog food, shotgun shells, a new hunting jacket and a supply of Dago Red.

Shorty's request for government money was quickly processed. The approval notification advised him of a typographic error in his application. Inadvertently, he typed "$1,000" when, obviously, he meant "$5.000".

When Shorty received the check for $6,000, he immediately embarked on his study. He bought a dog from Honest Carl Wussow. Honest Carl was a local used car dealer who had taken the dog in trade as part payment for an automobile. Honest Carl told Shorty the dog was part English Pointer and part Japanese Dissa.

Shorty knew the Pointer was a good hunter, but he had never heard of a Japanese Dissa. Honest Carl told him the Dissa was used in Japan to find and flush storks from rice fields and sushi groves and other Japanese type places where the birds occurred. With both English and Japanese hunting dog blood lines, Shorty guessed the animal would be a natural-born hunter.

Honest Carl didn't hunt. Shorty was sure he had no idea of the value of an animal bred for the specialized purpose of hunting birds. Shorty happily paid a thousand dollars for the dog. By the time he paid for a collar and a bell, flea powder (a lot of flea powder) and various veterinary bills to have the animal de-wormed and de-ticked and de-manged, Shorty still had enough left to lay in a nice supply of Dago Red and pay his own doctor bill. (Shorty got a bad case of the mange from the dog.)

The attempts to train the mixed breed dog were not entirely successful. It may have been the Dissa's blood line. The Japanese dog's ancestors had been bred to run into and around fields and paddies. The Dissa had been developed for the purpose of chasing hungry cranes and storks out of the growing rice. To perform that function, the Dissa was a lone hunter, conditioned to protect large expanses of land. The presence of a hunter to direct the dog's movements was unnecessary. As a result, the dog could not be trained to hunt within the range of a 12 ga. shotgun. Shorty claimed it couldn't be trained to hunt within the range of a .308 deer rifle.

That was not the dog's only problem. Throughout the centuries, the Dissa had been taught to find and flush cranes and storks. Shorty's dog would hunt only long legged birds - like Sand Hill Cranes, Cattle Egrets and Herons. Moreover, the dog would not hold a point. It consistently frightened the cranes and egrets into flight long before Shorty could get close enough to fire a shot. The dog could not be trained to hold a bird until the hunter arrived.

Nevertheless, Shorty persevered. He continued his unsuccessful attempts to train the dog until his supply of Dago Red had been completely consumed. Then he admitted failure and sold the dog. Shorty believes the dog's new owner changed its name to CUMHEARYEWNOGUDSOB. At least, that's what the new owner called out whenever he tried to get the dog to come back to somewhere close to shotgun range.

Shorty's experiment proves any attempts to produce a hunting dog by cross breeding an English Pointer with a Japanese Dissa will produce nothing more than a Dissa Pointer.

The Madness of Peabody

It was after five in the afternoon when I visited Major Nathaniel Peabody. I intended to invite him to an evening at his favorite German restaurant. "Oh, it's you," he said as he opened the door and ushered me into his apartment. Paying no further attention to me, he returned to his wing backed chair and began to act in a peculiar manner.

Without a single word or any kind or acknowledgment of my presence, he drew his lips into a small open circle, sucked air through his nose and began to snort. "I can't seem to get it right," he said abstractly and then repeated those strange sounds.

I became alarmed. To say the least, his behavior was preposterous. Some rational explanation would, I assumed, be forthcoming. I sat, patiently waiting for that explanation, while he continued his snorting, changing the pitch from tenor to bass and the rhythm from staccato to slow funereal phrasings, but always shaking his head in dissatisfaction. "I just can't seem to get it right," he repeated aloud.

"Can't seem to get what just right?" I ventured. Apparently my question didn't register with him. He paid no attention to it. Instead, the Major glanced in my general direction and said: "The sun has been over the yard arm for a goodly time, young man." This was 'Peabodyese'. It translates into English as: "I believe it is time for a dollop of the single malt."

I went to the kitchen, retrieved the liter of The Macallan from its hiding place beneath the sink and was in the act of getting ice cubes from the refrigerator when I again heard a series of disgusting grunts coming from the living room. It was disconcerting.

What was even more disturbing was Peabody's refusal to accept my invitation to dinner. He said he was too busy. Busy doing what? Frightening me with his dreadful noises? I've known the man for years and he seldom, if ever, neglected a chance to enjoy ox joint and sauerkraut - to be followed by cigars and libations. Something was terribly wrong, but I was afraid to ask him about the reason for the snorts periodically punctuating the rest of our late-afternoon conversations.

I could not help but recall my experiences in the practice when I was newly out of law school. Clients were hard to find and I was happy to have any customers - even when it meant representing poor, confused creatures at Commitment Hearings. Recalling the bizarre actions of those clients, I now wondered if Major Peabody might be losing his grip on reality. My concern about his state of mind led me to believe he needed help.

After a sleepless night, I determined my course of action. I would seek the assistance of Doctor Carmichael. Though he was a medical doctor, I suspected he would be able to recommend a competent psychiatrist and, I hoped, assume the responsibility of convincing the Major to see him. I met with the doctor on the following morning.

In answer to Doctor Carmichael's question, I told him I suffered from no noxious disease and that it was the Major who needed help. The doctor sighed, shook his head and said: "I'm sorry. I will not go bail for him. You're the attorney. You get him out of whatever mess he's gotten into."

I hastened to assure him the police were not after Peabody. I told him I believed the Major might be taking leave of his senses. Doctor Carmichael removed his glasses, slowly shook his head and admitted he had long suspected this day would come.

When I told him how the Major insisted on making those dreadful sounds, Carmichael asked if I had mentioned my concerns to Peabody. I answered in the negative and reported my fear of the possible reaction if, to put it bluntly, I told the Major I thought he was a nut case and in need of professional help.

"That is, indeed, a risk," the doctor agreed. "The medical journals have printed studies classifying reactions to such accusations. Some cuckoos calmly accept it as fact. Others immediately kill their spouses and expect me to get them off by giving evidence of their insanity. Of course, some deny it. Strangely enough, some of them consider their nuttiness to be a qualification for public office. The House of Representatives and the Senate are full of them. Just look at the ridiculous gun control legislation they propose.

"You were wise to keep your suspicions to yourself. I'll take over from here. In two days, Peabody and I are leaving for a duck hunt in Florida. I promise I will carefully observe him and take appropriate steps if involuntary commitment is indicated."

* * * * *

Their truck was parked in the pines on the adjacent higher ground. It was mid-morning and the two men were walking from the edge of the Florida marsh. Major Peabody carried the gunny sacks of decoys. Doc Carmichael followed carrying the shotguns and a bag slung over his shoulder. It was heavy. It contained their daily limit of ducks. The dog didn't carry anything.

"I've never seen anything like it, Nate. Whatever possessed

you to do it?"

"Elementary, my dear Doctor. It is simply a result of my keen observation skills, my unrivalled imagination and my superior intelligence."

"Please don't continue. I think I'm going to throw up."

"All right. Do your best to concentrate and I'll try to explain it. When all is said and done, the primary motivating forces controlling all forms of life are food and sex."

"Right."

"Usually we can't hunt during the bird mating seasons."

"Right."

"That means we must rely on food to attract ducks."

"Right."

"You've hunted turkeys on Tom Rosenow's land in Wisconsin. Do you remember his automatic corn feeder and how the turkeys were conditioned to appear within minutes after it had gone off and scattered the corn around its base?"

"Yes."

"Why did the birds behave that way?"

"Food?"

Peabody shook his head in disbelief. "No, you idiot. If it were merely food, the turkeys would nest under the feeder and never move away from it. Search your defective memory for Pavlov's experiment. The animal salivated when Pavlov rang a bell. The turkeys came to Tom's feeder when they heard the sound of the automatic feeding machine. It was the sound that told them the corn had been scattered.'

"I see, but…"

Peabody held up his hand, silencing the doctor, and continued his explanation. "For decades Clevis Dewlap and his Florida progenitors have owned this land and grown hogs on it for food and for a cash crop."

"So?"

"They raised the hogs by turning them loose in the woods and letting them fend for themselves. It's still a common practice. The hogs usually feed on acorns and other wild foodstuffs. In addition, some farmers will feed them corn to fatten them up. Clevis is one of them. He brings bags of corn down here and dumps them out next to the marsh. It's where the hogs come for water. Clevis has no use for an automatic feeder. The ducks, therefore, have no machine-created whirring sound to advise them precisely when the corn has been put out for the hogs."

Carmichael captured the concept. "Aha," he said. "I see. I see. That's why you kept grunting and snorting. It's the kind of sound a hog makes when it's eating. Your snorting was a duck call. It told the ducks Clevis brought corn to the edge of the marsh and the hogs were eating it. That's why they decoyed so well."

Peabody smiled.

So did Carmichael. "Let's not tell your lawyer," he said. "We'll keep him guessing. It will drive him nuts."

Genetics

The end-of-the-month ritual was about to be observed. Major Nathaniel Peabody would be short of funds. I would come to his apartment. He would insult me and complain about the terms of his Spendthrift Trust. I would provide a dinner at Bookbinders. We'd return to his apartment to continue our conversations and enjoy an evening libation or two.

The conversations with Major Peabody always concern subjects closely associated with shotgun hunting. They were matters in which I have a complete lack of experience, knowledge or interest. The word "conversation" is not entirely accurate. Peabody did the conversing. My own participation is limited. I am put in charge of listening and occasionally saying things like "How very interesting" or "I never thought of it that way" or "Do go on".

(Like Pavlov's dog, I have also been conditioned to mix and deliver another single malt Scotch and water whenever I hear the Major clink the ice cubes in his empty glass.)

I always hope Peabody will find a subject of more wide-spread, popular interest - some subject I could talk about - like recent Supreme Court decisions, or the taxation of revocable trusts agreements. It always proves to be a forlorn hope. The Major talks about dogs or shotguns or game birds and, from time to time, the unconstitutionality of Spendthrift Trusts and the need for a law providing for the incarceration of attorneys who prepare them.

This time, when I arrived at his apartment, the Major's

greeting showed him to be in an unusually cheerful frame of mind.

"Good afternoon, Counselor. I hope you've had a pleasant day keeping widows and orphans from enjoying the benefits of being trust beneficiaries. Come in. Sit. It's a beautiful day." It wasn't a beautiful day. It was cold and gray and icy and windy.

"You seem to be in good humor," I observed.

"I am, indeed," he answered. "I've just finished reading an article about chickens. What an inspiring dissertation." It looked like Peabody had selected the subject matter for the day's educational lecture. I resigned myself to the ordeal.

"Ah, Prairie Chickens," I said in a failed attempt to show enthusiasm and then recounted the full extent of my knowledge of the bird. "I believe they were first described by Lewis and Clark during the Voyage of Discovery. I think they are found in western states. Can you tell me about them? Are you planning a hunting trip?"

"No, no. no," Peabody corrected. "You don't understand. I don't mean Prairie Chickens. I mean that lesser kind - Rhode Island Reds - Plymouth Rock Whites. You know. The kind that go cluck, cluck, cluck and lay eggs."

This was a peculiar departure from our time honored ritual. I wondered if the Major was ill or if the terrible weather had affected his mind. I decided to ignore his aberration, hoping it was no more than a temporary condition.

I went to the kitchen, intending to calm him with a single malt Scotch and water. Peabody followed close behind me. He put his hand to his forehead, then waved both arms in the air and exclaimed "An epiphany, Counselor. An epiphany. Bless the scientists. Bless them all. What fantastic potentials."

"Chickens?" I questioned, in more than mild disbelief.

"No. Not chickens, you idiot. Recombinant genetics."

"Oh, I understand," I said, having no idea of what he was

talking about.

"I was bored silly," the Major continued in lively tones. "This damned weather is so depressing. I tried to concentrate on duck hunting, but it was no use. I read an article claiming biologists can fool around with a chicken's genes and produce a bird with four or six or even eight drumsticks. It's a miraculous scientific achievement. It portends a future beyond my most optimistic projections."

Peabody surprised me. What a refreshing change. He was directing his attentions to the consideration of one of humanity's most tragic problems. Finally, I could spend an evening engaging him in the serious discussion of a subject not directly associated with dogs or shotguns or hunting.

"I see. I see," I exclaimed with unfeigned enthusiasm. "You mean the world's starvation problems can be minimized by producing chickens with eight legs. More food for the undernourished through genetic manipulations. The potential is, indeed, mind boggling. What an interesting subject..."

"No, you don't see," Peabody interrupted. "I'm thinking of something much, much more important. If those marvelous genetic engineers can add legs to a chicken, just think of what they can do for duck hunters. They could give me an extra pair of arms."

I'm afraid my jaw dropped. Peabody paid no attention to my reaction.

"How often have far away ducks circled my blind, waiting for the time when, cold and shivering, I hold my mug in one hand and, with the other, begin to pour coffee from the thermos? Consistently, this is the precise moment when the ducks will buzz my decoys, secure in the knowledge that I will pour hot coffee on my crotch - an act that always distracts me from picking up my shotgun and firing at them.

"Revenge. Revenge," he said through clenched teeth.

"Once the scientists have fitted me with an extra set of arms, those damned ducks will pay for their insolence. When they buzz my decoys, I'll be able to pick up my shotgun, drop a pair of them and, at the same time, fill my coffee mug without spilling a drop. They'll be dead in the water before they know what hit them."

Then another thought occurred to him. He smiled and said: "Perhaps these magnificent scientists can steal a dog's DNA, inject it into me and endow me the animal's ability to smell." The Major paused for a few seconds before he looked up and explained. "I don't mean giving me the ability to smell like a dog after it has rolled in a dead fish or some equally odiferous material. I mean the dog's ability to use its nose. It's hundreds of times more sensitive than a human's."

The Major was pleased by the prospects of recombinant genetics. He smiled as he discovered another benefit. "Just think of the advantage I'll have. I won't need a hunting dog. I'll know where the grouse and pheasants are long before other hunters have so much as a suspicion. Oh, brave new world. Just think of it, Counselor. I can have the eye of an eagle, the hearing of a deer, the grouse's ability to eat poisonous mushrooms."

The end-of-month ritual had not been disturbed. I took a sip of my Scotch and water and assumed my usual responsibilities. "How very interesting," I said "Do go on."

Justice

It was the evening of the last day of the month. I was in a grouse camp in the UP, prepared to deliver Major Nathaniel Peabody's Spendthrift Trust remittance. For the benefit of the uninitiated, "UP" refers to Michigan's Upper Peninsula. It's a thinly populated area and its inhabitants are called "Yoopers".

After a dinner of pan fried grouse, the Major and his three Yooper hunter friends retired to the other side of the combination kitchen/dining/recreation area of the cabin for libation and recreation. Of course, every one of the Yoopers knew I was a Philadelphia attorney and the conversation turned to matters jurisprudential.

Major Peabody took no part in the discussion. He was occupied removing burrs, stick-tights and other unwanted clinging weed seeds from the long haired ears and withers of an English Pointer a/k/a Lothario. The dog sat next to him with muzzle laid on his lap and eyes closed, obviously enjoying the procedure which involved plenty of ear scratching.

The Major had an ulterior motive. Since there were six men and only two dogs, each dog had to work with its owner and two other hunters. Peabody hoped Lothario would show his appreciation during the following day's hunts by working close to him rather than ranging in front of all of the hunters.

One of the Yoopers - the one called Pete - started the discussion. "How could they let that Hollywood celebrity off," he asked me. "No question about it. He killed her. They should have found him guilty and hung him. The miserable SOB deserved it"

"The jury found him Not Guilty and that was that." I answered.

"That was what comes when you put a stupid judge, an incompetent District Attorney and a biased jury together," another Yooper, Charlie, explained.

"Stupid judges and incompetent District Attorneys?" I questioned, surprised by the man's accusation.

"Oh, yes," Pete answered. "I suspect it's a universal problem. It certainly is a common condition up here in the UP. You see," he explained, "some young attorney, fresh from law school, comes here and hangs out his shingle. Of course, he doesn't know much. He can't find the handles on the court house door and runs the risk of starving to death for lack of business.

"We take pity on the poor fellow and elect him District Attorney, thereby providing him with an income. If he is smart, as soon as he learns the basic procedures of his profession, he quits the DA job and quickly builds a successful private practice. If he is stupid, we keep electing him District Attorney. Then when another young lawyer comes to town, we send the stupid DA up to the judge's bench and elect the new guy to the vacated DA position."

"Don't the other lawyers object to having to practice before incompetent judges," I inquired.

"Of course not," Charlie answered. "Lawyers don't want smart judges. They want ones they can easily fool. Up here we have stupid judges and incompetent DAs, but we have unbiased juries and that is all you really need to dispense justice."

"And since the judge and the DA are both dummies, justice depends on the good sense of the jury," I said, completing his thought. "Have you ever been on a jury," I asked.

"Oh, sure," Pete said. "I was on one just last month. The Game Warden caught Aksel Jorgenson with too many ducks. We all call the Warden "Officer Dog" because he's such a miserable SOB. At the trial he got on the stand and testified the ducks were flying and he heard a lot of shooting at Rice Lake. He sneaked over there and found Aksel's pick-up truck parked behind John Martin's cabin. Then he hid in the shrubbery behind John's place and watched the duck blind Aksel had built out in the lake.

"He knew Aksel was a good shot and it didn't take long before he saw him drop a number of birds and then begin to pick up his decoys. Officer Dog watched Aksel paddle back to John's cabin and saw him take seven Bluebill from the skiff and put them in the front seat of his pick-up.

"Officer Dog was disappointed. Seven Bluebill were the legal limit. His spirits rose when he saw Aksel walk back to the cabin, take the cover off the garbage can next to the back door and remove another seven birds.

"Aksel told a slightly different story. He testified he shot his limit of ducks, brought them to shore and was just about to drive away when he became curious about that garbage can. He opened it and, too his amazement, he saw all those ducks inside it. He took them out to count them and got arrested. He thought maybe Office Dog put them there to trap him."

"The judge told us it wasn't necessary for the Warden to actually see Aksel shoot those other seven birds. Mere possession of them was enough to convict.

"That gave us jurors a problem. Aksel had a wife and five kids. Moreover, Officer Dog was such a miserable SOB. He had a well established reputation for making silly arrests. He had given almost all of the jury panel citations for such insignificant violations as not having an approved life jacket in a boat or shooting too may partridge. He even gave one to

Charlie for inadvertently shooting an out-of-season deer."

Charlie vigorously nodded his head in agreement and added: "The miserable SOB."

Then Pete slowly shook his head back and forth. "He gave me one for failure to have an up-to-date fishing license. It was only six years old."

"In Aksel's case, justice was served. We came to the conclusion Aksel never really had possession of those last seven ducks. We found him Not Guilty. Office Dog looked forward to confiscating Aksel's ducks, shotgun, skiff, decoys and pick-up truck. He was mad as hell when we let Aksel go. We were all happy to frustrate Officer Dog. The miserable SOB deserves lots of frustrations."

"Tell him about the time you were on the jury when Daisy shot Ole," Pete said and Sven took over.

"Oh, yeah, I remember that one. Ole came home drunk and beat up Daisy again. He did it all the time. Then he started eating dinner and passed out at the table. Daisy went to his arsenal and picked out a shotgun. It was the 28 inch barreled, 16 gauge, full choke, Iver Johnson Champion single shot, probably built in 1945. Yeah, that was the one she took. Ole always claimed he only used it for grouse, but a lot of slugs went thru that barrel whenever a grouse season deer appeared before him.

"I suppose Daisy wanted to make sure. She loaded the shotgun with double aught buck shot and blew Ole's head off. She admitted pulling the trigger. Her planning made it obvious the whole affair was premeditated. We came to a verdict and could have left the jury room is less than an hour. It was after eleven o'clock, so we delayed until noon in order to get the county to provide us with a free meal. We got chicken and pizza. It was good.

"At one o'clock when court reconvened, we found Daisy

Not Guilty by reason of Temporary Insanity. Ole beat her up a lot and never bothered to repay any of the money some of us lent to him. Daisy was overjoyed by our verdict. She came to the jury box and thanked each one of us individually. When she got to the foreman, I heard him whisper in her ear: "Ole deserved it. He was miserable SOB".

"It seems to me," I ventured, "that people considered being miserable SOBs have a difficult time of it in the UP."

"We do our best to keep it a nice place to live. Remember that attorney?" Sven asked. "The crooked one? The one who charged so much? The one who couldn't shoot straight?"

"Oh yes." Pete answered. "He was a miserable SOB. We fixed his clock good and proper. We had to get rid of him so we sent him to Congress. Now he lives in Washington and doesn't bother us, except when he comes back to campaign for re-election."

I hope no Yooper ever thinks I am a miserable SOB.

A Social Animal

The sun was rising when I retrieved Major Peabody's shotgun and baggage from the airport carousel and loaded them into my auto. He seemed darkly preoccupied and was not his usual ebullient self. The trip from northern Minnesota to Minneapolis and the night flight to Philadelphia must have tired him.

It was Saturday and I had no real need to go to the office. "Why don't we go to my place" I suggested. "I'll fix breakfast and drop you off at your apartment after we've eaten."

A monosyllable and a short up-down nod indicated the Major's agreement. It also confirmed my guess. He was definitely not in one of his better moods.

* * * * *

I added more coffee to the percolator and plugged it in. The Major likes his morning coffee strong and black. He also likes hash browns made from scratch. By the time the potato was grated, the coffee was ready and I took a mug to him.

"Coffee? Coffee?" he asked, just as if he'd never heard of it before. "Take it away. I'm not going to drink coffee anymore", he said with some emphasis. "Have you got anything else?" It was too early for it, but I suggested a high ball. Peabody declined and asked for water. This was, indeed, strange. He seldom took water straight, usually preferring to drink it with a single malt Scotch whisky. He claimed it removed the water's unpleasant taste.

During breakfast, he came out of his brown study and began to talk.

"Frankly," he said, "Mother Nature's track record has not been too good. For example, she developed dinosaurs. They had great bodies, but she messed up with their brains which were decidedly second rate. When that experiment failed, she wasn't even successful when trying to wipe everything out and start over again. Sharks, horse shoe crabs and cockroaches (none of them noted for high intelligence quotients) were all able to outsmart her and survive.

"Then she searched around for a successor species to run the planet. She considered and quickly rejected the petitions of the ants, the fish and the pterodactyls, probably because they didn't have opposable thumbs. She settled on the anthropoids. It may be too early to judge the success of her attempt to develop the Homo sapiens as an appropriate ruler of her earthly domain, but I see unmistakable signs that it, too, has been a terrible and a dismal failure.

"I'll bet she's sorry she put her money on the Homo sapiens. I suspect she has finally discovered him to be a worthless creature. Natural disasters like famine, flood, earthquake and volcanic eruptions as well as unnatural disasters like liberal political philosophies all come to mind as examples of the her initial attempts to get us to follow the Great Auk into extinction.

"Once we're all out of the way, I believe she'll select the squirrels as our successors. They are smarter than we are. After all, we are unable to deal with such simple problems as keeping them out of our bird feeders. Squirrels, I hasten to remind you, have never been known to create an Inquisition, start a major war, or treat their fellows in thoughtless and inconsiderate manners."

"Oh, come now, Major", I said, "Don't give up on your

species. Look at the brighter side. In spite of everything, there is a basic goodness in the human character. Mankind is doing all right. We may not be perfect, but over the eons, we've evolved from abjectly primitive beasts to advanced social beings."

The attempt to raise his spirits failed. Peabody laid the cigar in the ash tray and looked at me. After a moment he said: "A social being? Thoughtful and considerate of his fellow man? Do you really think so?" He emphasized the word 'really'. I answered in the affirmative and he called for a dictionary.

"Here", he said. He put his finger on the word and read it and the definition. "Social. Marked or characterized by friendliness or geniality enjoyed in the company of others.' Friendliness enjoyed in the company of others," he repeated.

"Sounds accurate to me," I said.

"Aha," Peabody answered and slammed the tome shut. "There is little friendliness or geniality within the character of the Homo sapiens. Let me tell you what just happened in Minnesota.

"When a new man is invited into our grouse camp, we try to treat him in a friendly and genial manner during his initiation period. His sense of humor and the stability of his character are tested. The newcomer to our Minnesota camp was a miscreant named Freddie Campbell. At first, he showed the qualities you mention, but the indication of his true nature was shown by the chili he brought to camp.

"In Campbell's chili, it was easy to recognized Hungarian paprika, Caribbean hot sauce, Cayenne peppers and jalapeños, separating occasional bits of venison, onions and kidney beans. I'm convinced he got his recipe from Lucretia Borgia who used it to poison those who offended her. Before serving it, he advised us to have no fear because it had been set in the open air for three days and all noxious gases had escaped.

"My hunting companions' praise of Campbell's chili was somewhat muted. They mumbled comments like: 'I wouldn't expose my worst enemy to this chili.' 'A starving hyena would run from it.' 'No self respecting buzzard would be seen near it,' and 'The only ecologically responsible way to deal this stuff is to bury it, deeply, in solid granite, the same way they handle contaminated atomic waste.'

"By the time Campbell finished the dishes (another of the newcomer's duties), his bottle of Wild Turkey was empty and in a friendly, but straight forward manner, he was criticized for (a) not bringing George Dickel and (b) not bringing enough of it.

"And so our genial initiation ceremonies for the new man progressed throughout the hunt. He prepared all breakfasts, tended the fire, filled the wood box and kept the cabin 'man clean'. These responsibilities claimed all of his mornings, but he was able to hunt in the afternoons because lunch consisted of the chili (which remained in the pot, uneaten) and a few sandwiches. He didn't have to spend much time in luncheon dish washing and general clean up.

"In the afternoons, when Campbell was hunting with us, he continued to receive our same pleasant attentions. He wandered a bit to the right and left a gap in the line of hunters as we advanced through a new growth of popple. He caught unmitigated hell and was threatened with having to wear a dog's shock collar if he ever went off course again. You can imagine what happened when he missed a shot.

"After dinner, charges of allowing a bird to escape were brought. I was appointed to defend him. I proved he was clumsy and inept and was hunting with the safety off when the gun accidentally discharged - a crime less heinous than missing a bird.

"Nevertheless, he was found guilty. His name and the date of the crime were written on a toilet seat, where it joined the list of those who committed the same sin during previous hunts. Then, in accordance with camp rule # 46, he wore the seat around his neck for the balance of the evening.

"At breakfast, yesterday morning, Campbell was told he passed his apprenticeship and was now a fully fledged member of the camp. Did he display any of the friendliness and geniality you assign to the Homo sapiens? No, he did not. In spite of the cordial and considerate treatment we so generously extended to him, he was neither friendly nor genial.

"Just as soon as he received our collective stamp of approval, he showed his true colors. He asked "Do I get to hunt every morning?"

"That's right," was our response.

"Everybody pitches in on the chores?"

"That's right."

"Well, that's just great," he said. "And to show my appreciation, I'll no longer use my dirty socks to strain the grounds out of your morning coffee."

The Dread Disease

For as long as I've known Major Nathaniel Peabody he's never experienced a day of illness. I catch cold and get the sniffles every year and whenever a new kind of Oriental flu bug gets off the boat on the West Coast it will hurry to Philadelphia and immediately make its way to my digestive tract.

During such epidemics, the Major doesn't even sneeze. When I complain, he smiles and accuses me of hypochondria. The microbes, the viruses and the fungi that attack the rest of us seem to be afraid of him. I've often heard his say: "I don't get ulcers. I give them". I'm convinced he has the constitution of an ox.

Peabody, however, explains his good health by declaring the medicinal effects of cigar smoke and aged single malt Scottish whisky. He claims they quickly polishes off all toxic and noxious matter that may have been so ill-advised as to enter his system. When he suggested this theory to his friend, Doctor Carmichael, the medico countered by suggesting the Major's various dissipations had softened his brain, or, as he put it "what is left of what was, at best, a substandard and poorly wired organ."

The only explanation making any sense is this: During the Major's shotgunning trips to the various strange places he frequents, he must have come in contact with all known diseases and developed immunity to every one of them. Apparently, he has developed the ability to avoid illness. I wish he had developed the ability to plan for his future. I don't mean planning for some event expected to happen in the distant future. I mean planning the use of his more than adequate guaranteed income in such a manner that it will last for a full calendar month.

During the end-of-month days when he is penniless (often), it has become my practice to provide him with dinners. This month was an exception. It was only a bit past mid-month and Peabody was already broke. He had gone on an expensive African safari, returning with a financial reserve of nothing more than pocket change.

On Thursday we ate at Bookbinders. Today it was time for another meal. I telephoned him. You can imagine my surprise when Peabody refused my offer. This was one of the very few times he declined an invitation to dinner. You can imagine my further surprise when he told me he was sick.

It wasn't merely a temporary "feeling a bit under the weather" indisposition. Peabody told me he called Doctor Carmichael who ordered him to the Emergency Room where he performed several tests. The Major told me no more. He abruptly ended our phone conversation. Frankly I was worried about him. I called Doctor Carmichael.

I was told Peabody became exposed to some rare virus during his recent hunting expedition to Zimbabwe. Doctor Carmichael assured me I had no cause for concern. According to the Disease Control Center in Atlanta, the disease, though quite contagious, was not life threatening.

It would run its course in four days. In the meantime, it would, unfortunately, cause him maximum discomfort - headache, runny nose, nausea, a stomach able to hold few solids, fever and extreme dizziness, together with frequent and explosive attacks of diarrhea. Now I understood why the Major has so abruptly ended our phone conversation.

I questioned the doctor and was told medical science had

yet to find an effective antidote Due to the report of the "quite contagious" characteristic of Peabody's dreaded disease, I felt it prudent to forebear any personal visit to him. My firm represents a number of casualty insurance companies. We had just finished a successful defense against a slip-and-fall damage action brought against a local restaurant. The chef owed us a favor. I prevailed upon him to prepare and deliver meals to the Major.

On Monday afternoon, I was drafting the wording of an intricate testamentary trust when the light on my office intercom flashed. My secretary, Charlotte, informed me: "Major Peabody is here". Her tone of voice translated the words into her intended meaning of: "That terrible Major person wants to waste some more of your time"

Charlotte doesn't like Major Peabody. She thinks he is a male chauvinist. She believes he is insensitive to the point of not even being aware of the struggle for equality between the sexes. Her assessment is probably accurate. Personally, I believe Charlotte is disturbed because the gods have, so far, refused to visit the plague or some other appropriate punishment on the Major as retribution for his callous disregard of women's rights, gun control, shaving the whales and other holy causes.

"Shall I tell him you cannot be disturbed?" she asked, hoping for an affirmative response.

"No, Charlotte. Please ask him to come in." It was time for a break and I wanted to see if the Major had regained his health.

I was pleased to find Peabody was, indeed, all right. In spite of his four day ordeal, his color was back and he was in good spirits. He thanked me for the courtesy of the catering. "Most kind of you, my boy," he said. "You have no idea of how impossible would be the task of trying to prepare a meal when the stomach, the sinuses and the intestines are all in revolt. When one orifice is not erupting, another one is. Your kindness is truly appreciated." Then he asked a disturbing question. "I presume you have made arrangements with the caterer to provide a similar service for yourself?"

"Oh," I questioned in return.

"Surely Doc Carmichael told you? Surely you know how contagious that disease is? Didn't he tell you the dreaded sickness strikes thirteen days after initial exposure? We had dinner together at Bookbinders. Wasn't it about tens days ago. You're going to catch whatever I had in another few days."

I sat there with my mouth wide open. Of course, I knew I was going to get whatever terrible disease the Major just survived.

Peabody slowly shook his head. "I don't envy you my boy. I know what you must face. It's quite debilitating. Look on the brighter side. It's only four days. Then you'll be able to leave the confines of your apartment. You're young and you're strong. I believe you'll live through it."

* * * * *

Major Nathaniel Peabody left the law offices of Smythe, Hauser, Engels and Tauchen. He descended to the lobby. As he left the building, he was joined by Doctor Carmichael.

"Everything go OK, Nate?"

"It went as smooth as silk, Doc. In another few days, he believes he's going to get whatever you told him I had. He thinks he won't be able to leave the bathroom for another four days. He even called the caterer to get chicken broth and crackers delivered to him."

"How about your check?"

"He's convinced he won't be able to deliver it to me. It's

due in five days and I told him you were taking me to South Dakota. He made me promise not to tell anyone. I've got the check in my pocket.

"I'll never drink another cup of chicken broth in this lifetime, but it was worth it. The duck hunting is great in Nicaragua and we're leaving tomorrow."

Warning Signs

It was in Upper Michigan. The Ruffed Grouse season was in full swing. The two German Wirehairs had performed brilliantly during the day. The evening meal (grouse, of course, with wild mushrooms) had been delicious. The dishes were washed and the libations and cigars had been distributed. What more could a man want. A poker game?

Nathaniel Peabody, Doc Carmichael, two Yoopers and a Troll were at the table.

For the benefit of the uninitiated, a Yooper is someone who lives in the U P - Michigan's Upper Peninsula. A Troll is a someone who lives in Lower Michigan, south of the bridge that crosses the juncture of Lake Michigan and Lake Huron and connects the two parts of the State. In other words, a Troll is a creature who lives below the bridge.

The game was Seven Card Stud. One of the Yoopers was dealing. He held the deck, waiting for the bets as the Troll waved his hand to disburse a bit of the cigar smoke. The players had five cards, two down and three up. The Major already had a heart flush. He could read no warning signs indicating anyone might be working on a full house. Peabody hoped no one would recognize the danger of his three heart face cards.

"Old camp cooks should be respected," the Major observed as he tried to distract his companions from recognizing the threat. "If you overlook their criminal records, their dreadful diseases and their slovenly ways, they can be convenient additions to hunting camps."

"I know what you're up to," Charlie Ainsworth said. Charlie was one of the Yoopers and the camp cook. "You're complimenting me because you want me to get more snacks." He had a Queen up and he bet a dollar. Then he went into the kitchen area and returned with another bag of Fritos. He dumped them into the empty bowls.

The younger man at the table was the Troll. He threw a dollar into the pot and voiced an objection. "Junk food," It almost sounded like swearing. He refused the Fritos and took a trail food bar from his pocket. After a few unsuccessful attempts to open the plastic, he ripped it apart with his teeth and took a bite from it.

"This is a multi-grained food supplement," he announced. "It's been scientifically engineered to provide the very best nutritional elements needed by the human body. It's good for you. It's a wonder any of you old guys have managed to live so long - what with all the poisonous stuff you eat."

Peabody again checked his hole cards, trying to leave the impression they were so valueless he had forgotten what they were. He slowly shook his head, muttering, "I don't know why I do things like this," and he dropped a dollar into the good sized and growing pot. Charlie Ainsworth picked up the plastic wrapper the young man had dropped on the table. "I tried one of these once," Charlie admitted. "If I remember correctly, it tasted like artificially sweetened saw dust."

Charlie read through the list of ingredients. "Let's see - the crust contains potassium bicarbonate, simulated flavors, micro crystalline cellulose, carrageen and guar gum. Does anyone have the vaguest idea of what they are? The filling is made of glycerol, more simulated flavors, sodium alginate, sodium citrate, calcium phosphate, methylcellulose, malic acid and coloring. Glucose and fructose sugars and other stuff is scattered about, too. Doesn't sound very healthy to me. Must be another example of better living through chemistry."

Peabody joined the conversation. He was happy to do anything to distract the others. "I'll take my chances with ptomaine poisoning and liver flukes rather than expose my system to mixtures of soy beans and chemicals that taste like linoleum. I don't have to worry about cholera, typhoid, e-coli or the Black Plague. Aged single malt Scotch Whisky kills germs, fungi, bacteria and viruses."

The sixth card was dealt. It looked like the Troll was working on a straight. Peabody was happy to watch him raise Charlie's bet. Doc Carmichael dropped. And the Major continued his chatter.

"Homo sapiens has been around for half a million years. We've been successful and, so far, at least, have established mastery of all other forms of life. We've managed to attain our present elevated status by eating natural foods. Only recently has it been ..." he pause to find the right word "...enhanced, I think that's the term they use, by the addition of chemicals.

"True, our wiring, our plumbing and our muscular structure do wear out long before those of the Galapagos tortoises, the parrots and some kinds of trees, but, I hasten to point out, tortoises, parrots and trees don't add chemicals to their food."

"You could be right, Major," Charlie said. "But you'll have to admit it - modern food with all of its additives, makes a camp cook's life a lot easier. I don't have to peel potatoes anymore. I can get them straight out of the box. All I have to do is add some milk and butter and they don't taste bad."

The last card was dealt. Peabody glanced at the Troll. He had his hands on the pile of cash in front of him and he was looking to this right. It was a sign. He caught his straight and was waiting to pick up the pot. Charlie bet his Queens, the Troll raised, Peabody re-raised. Charlie and the silent Yooper both got the idea. They quickly dropped out of the competition. The Troll took the last raise. Peabody smiled and called.

"Chemicals can retard spoilage," he admitted. "And, yes, they may make the camp cook's life easier. However, you can't convince me they produce anything that's good to eat. I'd rather get my food from the Farmer's Market than from a DuPont factory. You've got to be smart enough to read the warnings. Have you ever read the label on that freeze dried flaked potato box?"

"I'll read it right now," Charlie answered. He left the table and went into the kitchen area. Peabody watched as he put on his glasses and took the box of instant potatoes flakes from the shelf. "Sodium Pyrophosphate," he read from the list of ingredients on the side of the box. "What's that stuff, Major?"

"Figure it our," Peabody told him. "What's a pyromaniac?"

Charlie scratched his head. He split the word in two. "Pyro maniac," he repeated. "That's a fire bug. Pyro must mean fire."

Peabody nodded in approval. "Right you are, Charlie. What do you know about phosphate?"

Charlie answered right away. "That's a fertilizer. You put it on the lawn to make the grass grow green," and slowly repeated the key words. "Pyro... Phosphate... fire... fertilizer... makes the grass grow green." He worked his way to a frightful conclusion. His eyes opened wide and his jaw dropped. "You know," he announced, "I believe somebody has been burning cow manure and putting it in the mashed potatoes."

Peabody tipped over his cards, showing the flush. The Troll looked sadly at his cards and tossed them into the discard pile.

* * * * *

There is a lesson to he learned. When Major Peabody pays

no attention to his cards and engages in irrelevant conversation, keep your hand on your wallet. Read the warning sign and muck your cards immediately.

Mephitis Mephitis

From the time he was big enough to carry a .410 ga. shotgun, Major Nathaniel Peabody has spent a substantial portion of his lifetime on lakes, in fields and in the woods, usually accompanied by a hunting dog and looking for pheasant, grouse, partridge, geese, ducks and various other kinds of game birds. In all such matters, he is both knowledgeable and experienced.

Before I was assigned the uncomfortable job of managing the Peabody Spendthrift Trust, my own experience with the fields and woods and lakes was limited to golf courses and water holes. The 12th hole bordered on a forested lot and my slice often took me into the woods where I spent considerable time searching for golf balls. (That experience served me well when the Major took me mushroom hunting. I had experience finding those little round things.)

On the first day of each and every month following my first meeting with Major Nathaniel Peabody, I have personally delivered his trust remittance check. During the days (and sometimes weeks) prior to that delivery, Peabody has spent his monthly allotment and is without funds. During these periods, I've provided him with numerous restaurant meals, bottles of the Macallan and boxes of imported cigars. In return, he has taught me what I know about the great out-of-doors.

I do not want to know about the great out-of-doors. Vicious snakes, quill throwing porcupines, wolves and hungry bears come to mind. Moreover, I'm not too sure I fully appreciate the teaching methods Major Peabody uses.

Early in our acquaintance, before I learned of Peabody's intense dislike of cocktail parties, a mutual friend, the lovely Stephanie, invited us to an afternoon affair at her Main Line country club. The Major agreed to attend only after subtle cajoling and, finally, outright threatening. Throughout the afternoon, he tried, desperately, to avoid showing it, but he was out of his element and quite ill at ease in the golf club and cocktail party ambient.

In an attempt to make him feel comfortable, the hostess searched until she found a guest who claimed to know all about the denizens of the forest. He was a college zoology Professor. She led him to the Major, performed the introduction and quickly escaped. They were left to endure each other's presence and painful conversation for at least fifteen minutes.

I came upon them in time to hear the stranger break an awkward silence with the information that Mephitis Mephitis was the Latin designation for the skunk. Another few more seconds of silence followed before Peabody unenthusiastically responded, "I didn't know that. Thank you for sharing it with me."

The Professor and the Major used my approach as an excuse for parting company. They did so with what appeared to be mutual relief. Frankly, I was impressed by the man. Surely, someone who could use terms like "Mephitis Mephitis" must be a true outdoorsman. Later, as we drove back to Philadelphia, I mentioned that admiration. Peabody snorted.

"I can't imagine what crime I committed in some previous existence to justify the agony I had to suffer this afternoon," he said. "Three hours in a cocktail party, compounded by a lengthy conversation with a pompous dilettante is infinitely more painful than being tortured by the Apaches and staked out over a hill of fire ants."

"Oh, come now, Major. Apparently, you don't like cocktail

parties," I guessed, "but the Professor surely must know a lot about skunks."

Again, Peabody snorted. "The only way to know wild life is through personal observation and association - not by way of watching laboratory tests, studying statistics, reading text books and memorizing Latin terms. I heard nothing from the fellow to suggest he had ever worn out a pair of boots or run from a moose in heat." He paused and then explained: "I mean the moose being in heat, not the Professor."

We drove on in silence for a few minutes while I thought about Peabody's comments. "Just how does one associate with a skunk?" I asked. "How does one get close enough to observe them? Both activities require a certain proximity to the animal. Given its reputation of being armed with the most powerful of chemical weaponry, both association and observation seem dangerous and not to be undertaken by a prudent man."

Peabody was ready for the question. "With the possible exception of college professors enjoying some large federal government polecat study grant, anyone who purposely seeks out association with a skunk should be confined to a lunatic asylum. I except university professors because, if they were to be put away, logic would require the Congressmen who created the study grant to be put away. If Congressmen are to be committed, the Sanity Commission should send the people who elected them to the same asylum. Half the population of the United States would be in padded cells."

Peabody didn't give me an opportunity to respond. He continued his educational lecture. "Contrary to general perception, the life of the hunter is not always a bed of roses. The shotgunner, in particular, puts himself in harm's way every time he engages in a hunt. Mosquitoes, wood ticks and No Trespassing signs are but a few of the challenges he must overcome. Of course, the skunk must be included within the list of perils.

"As you have suggested, hunters don't seek out skunks. They usually come upon them by accident. However, at times, the skunk seeks them out. I doubt there is a text book to instruct the student on where to empty the skillet containing grease from the breakfast bacon. The neophyte camp cook may merely pour it on the ground next to the kitchen tent door flap. He will do it only once. He will learn skunks like bacon grease.

"There is no treatise warning the shotgunner not to shoot a skunk with 7½ chilled bird shot. The shotgunner who does so will learn it upsets the skunk. He will also learn skunks have a very short fuse and, when upset, react instantaneously. The result of such a reaction will be indelibly etched in the hunter's memory.

"And there is the time honored adage: When a skunk comes into camp, everyone else leaves. Do you think that maxim was written by some college professor who, with a pad of paper and a pencil in hand, watched an experiment he set up in some Maine backwoods? I don't think so. I think it may have been a conclusion drawn by a group of shotgunners who had to evacuate a tent in the middle of the night when visitors with white stripes down their backs appeared in their midst to enjoy a meal of bacon grease.

"Is there a book explaining a method to safely get rid of skunks living under a cabin? I doubt it." The Major went silent and seemed to be considering the question. I considered it, too. If the skunks "went off", the cabin would be unlivable. Perhaps it would have to be burned down. After a few minutes, I broke the silence.

"Is there a way to get rid of them without the risk of what you call an 'instantaneous reaction?'" I inquired.

"I know of only one safe way," Peabody answered. Again, he was silent and offered no further explanation.

"And that is?" I prompted.

"It may seem strange to the uninitiated," he said, "Get some law books. Throw them under the cabin. It works. I've tried it."

"Major Peabody!" I exclaimed. "You don't expect me to believe a few law books placed under a cabin will drive out the skunks."

"No. Of course not, But the books will attract lawyers. When the lawyers crawl under the cabin, the skunks will leave."

* * * * *

Over the years I've tried, unsuccessfully to learn to avoid stepping into one of Major Peabody's bear traps.

Delusions

It had not been a pleasant day for the pheasant hunters. The rain started a half hour before sunrise and continued, alternating between light rains, drizzle and, occasionally, misting. Major Peabody rejected a ten o'clock invitation to go out into the mist with two young intrepid souls who picked up scatter guns, called a dog and left the cabin.

The men spent over an hour in the field before returning to the cabin. They were cold and soaked and representative of what Noah Webster's dictionary really meant when it defined the word "bedraggled". The only thing they got was a disgusted look from the Springer Spaniel reluctantly accompanying them.

"It's not a fit day for man or liberal," one of the men complained. "You and your bright idea," the other one snarled. They changed into dry clothing, wiped and oiled their weapons and toweled down the dog, while constantly complaining and expressing their feelings with short bad language phrases.

The hunters who stayed in the cabin knew any misconceived attempt to hunt anything but ducks in this kind of weather was an exercise in futility. Still, they shared their companions' unhappiness. The damned weather was keeping them from hunting, too. They took a modicum of solace from knowing they, at least, had remained dry.

Major Peabody voiced no complaints. He busied himself by ladling out bowls of venison chili simmering on the flat top of the pot bellied wood stove. The miserable hunters ate and became more comfortable, being warmed up by the heat from the wood stove and by the jalapeño peppers in the chili. Their complaints, however, continued unabated. Expletives, describing the rain and the wind, punctuated all conversation. By mid-afternoon, a sullen silence settled on the cabin.

The curse of the hunt destroying weather hung over the camp like a dense miasma. Peabody hoped the atmosphere would lighten up. He suggested a poker game, hoping it would direct his comrades' attentions from the weather and stop their constant complaining. Grudgingly, the other agreed. There wasn't anything better to do.

* * * * *

It was a very large pot. Not the kind used by the camp cook when he makes soup. It was the kind of pot developed when five poker players are each convinced they have the best hand and enthusiastically support their belief with bets.

A bit later, four disappointed players tossed their hand toward the dealer and made unhappy comment. "Lucky son of a deleted." "Damned rain." "I don't know why I play this game." "Damned rain." "You deal like old people romance. Not very well." "Damned rain." "I've done nothing to deserve such bad luck." "Don't forget the damned wind."

In contrast to their pessimistic muttering, the fifth man smiled and raked the chips from the pile heaped in the center of the table. As Peabody stacked his winnings, he observed: "Science and intelligence will eventually win out over ignorance and superstition."

It did nothing to improve his companions' attitudes. They stared - almost glared - at him. Noting their dour expressions, Peabody began a discourse designed to raise their spirits.

"Be not disheartened. Don't let the adversity of the moment

bother you. Your luck will change. Things are bound to get better."

One of the hunters added: "Before they get worse."

Peabody continued. "You have your choice. You can look on the bright side or you can look on the dark side. Life is much more pleasant if you adopt an optimistic attitude. Let me give you an example.

The folks who infest the TV talk shows are screaming: Killer Bees from Brazil will sting us to death, Global Warming will cause widespread starvation and a new Oriental Flu will decimate the population. The threat of the end of civilization as we know it is clearly set forth. The question is: Will you allow the frightful forecasts of irreversible, impending doom to ruin your life?

"I suggest you all adopt a positive attitude. Look on the bright side. Think of how much better off the country will be when the world's terrible over population problem has finally been solved.

"For eons, mankind's endeavors to advance the quality of life have been fueled by optimism. In the dim and distant past, our ancestors lived in trees. Falling out of bed had two disastrous consequences. It usually meant broken bones and, unless the tree dweller was quick enough to scramble back up the tree, it often meant being attacked and eaten by a Saber Toothed Tiger.

"The tree dweller didn't sit around the poker table wasting his time complaining about the quality of the cards he had been dealt or the rain or the wind that blew Aunt Tilly out of the tree and into the jaws of the tiger. They were optimists. They knew things would change for the better.

"It didn't take long before mankind left the trees and became cave dwellers. Soon someone picked up the thigh bone of a baboon and killed a tiger. As the optimistic tree dwellers

85

predicted, things got better." Peabody picked up the deck of cards and began to shuffle.

"What's your point, Major?"

"I've spent the day listening to your gloomy comments on the weather and the inexplicable bad luck you've experience here at the table. My point is this. When misfortune visits, you must acknowledge and convince yourself good fortune will soon return. You've got to remember the power of positive thinking. Your pessimism is destructive. Pessimists never feel the exhilaration of witnessing their positive thinking bring success.

"Seven Card Stud. A buck ante," Peabody announced and he dealt the cards. Peabody watched the expressions on the faces of the other hunters as they peeked at their hole cards. Two of them grimaced. One retained his poker face. The other slightly, only slightly, registered approval. The Major held two numbered clubs down and a Queen of diamonds up. A straight, a flush and all sorts of favorable combinations were possible.

As soon as the betting began, Peabody quickly mucked his cards. He knew his chances for improvement were no better than those of the enemy and two of the players appeared to hold hands superior to his. Optimism had nothing to do with his game. The Major was a realist. It was no time to take a chance.

Silently, Peabody thought: "*I hope they all bought that optimism and positive thinking nonsense. That sort of foolishness will encourage them to keep on betting long after a wise man would drop. I'm constantly amazed at how anyone can actually believe all that Pollyannaish, positive thinking silliness.*"

The Major looked out the cabin window. The sky was uniformly gray with no hint of sunshine or blue sky. It was raining again and the wind was picking up. It had all the characteristics of a three day rain.

As he turned back to the table and continued to deal cards to the other hunters, he thought: *"The rain will surely stop tonight. Tomorrow will be sunny. No wind. The pheasants will be out and that Springer Spaniel looks like a winner. I can just see those birds busting out from their cover. I can feel it in my bones. We're going to have an excellent hunt tomorrow. No question about it."*

Global Warming

The weather in Philadelphia during the month of February seldom produces expressions of joy from any of the city's inhabitants. The city in February can be an ordeal. It is a terrible ordeal for Major Nathaniel Peabody. His climate induced distress is grossly magnified when he is unable to find temporary relief by undertaking a hunting trip to some place where the sun shines mightily and overcoats are unknown. Unfortunately, Peabody's mismanagement of his finances often requires him to spend February in Philadelphia.

It was nearing the end of that month. I knew Peabody had frittered away his money and, as a result, had been apartment bound for nearly two weeks. Moreover, it had been an unreasonably cold, cold February. From my window in the Smythe, Hauser Engels & Tauchen law offices, I looked down at a street scene of frigid wind and snow. I knew how the Major would react to a cold and icy month in Philadelphia's gray and melancholy mid-winter.

He would be miserable. He would be despondent. He would be dejected. He would be in desperate need of cheering up.

Spending an evening with Peabody when he is in a foul mood is to be avoided at all cost. Nevertheless, I felt a powerful urge to lift his spirits and to invite him to an evening of conversation, good food and libation. My common sense demanded I immediately and completely disregard that impulse, but Peabody needed support. I decided to do my best to transform his attitude from dark dejection to one of rosy optimism.

I phoned the Major and, trying to be cheerful and upbeat, extended the invitation. Our brief conversation confirmed my assessment of his state of mind. The tone of his voice and every word he uttered spoke volumes. He was miserable. He was despondent. He was dejected. He was in desperate need of cheering up.

Nevertheless, my spirits were lifted by the knowledge that I was engaged in the charitable and benevolent undertaking of helping a friend overcome depression. It made me feel so good.

When I arrived at his apartment, I expected Peabody would be somber of feature, sour of temperament and an irritable dinner companion. I was not prepared for what ensued.

A smiling and animated Major Peabody met me at the door. He showed not the slightest sign of the grim melancholia he exuded during our brief phone conversation. "Come in, come in, Counselor," he bubbled. "So glad to see you. Isn't it a beautiful day?"

Beautiful day? It was freezing. The wind was blowing. The snow was piling up in drifts. Trying to raise his spirits may have been a praiseworthy endeavor, but it was beginning to lower mine. "You seem to be in a jovial mood," I ventured.

"I am, indeed," he answered, quite pleasantly. "I've just finished watching a fascinating program on television. What an inspirational event."

"Aha," I thought. "He's been watching one of those hunting programs. Undoubtedly, it has already pulled him out of his February brown study. My mission has already been accomplished. All I have to do is reinforce his current enthusiasm. Then I can cancel the dinner reservation and go home."

"Television is often a vast intellectual wasteland," I said.

"Those marvelous hunting programs are welcomed exceptions. Which one were you watching? Tell me about it. Are you planning a hunting trip?"

"No," he answered in lively tones. "I find it painful to watch someone hunting in his shirtsleeves in some sun drenched field while I'm enduring this damnedable weather. I turned on the TV, simply for the companionship of unintelligible background noise. My attention was captured by an engrossing exposition of the effects of global warming." His eyes widened as he exclaimed: "A profound enlightenment. It opened my mind. What fantastic events are in our future. Bless the environmental so-called scientists as well as their minions. Bless them all. Bless global warming."

Bless global warming? I couldn't believe my ears. It was the coldest day on record and Peabody was enthusing about global warming. I began to think the stress of February in Philadelphia had affected his mind. I considered calling Doctor Carmichael for immediate assistance in having him committed.

"You're sure you're not confusing global warming with global cooling?" I asked, hoping to gently nudge him back to reality. "The NASA people have been studying the temperature of the earth," I continued. "They claim it has been cooling, not warming. Qualified scientists report the last year as the coldest one in a decade. It's certainly very cold out there right now."

Peabody completely ignored my comment. He brushed it off, considering it to be nothing more than an inconvenient truth.

"All that ice and snow trapped on the polar cap and in Greenland will be released." He was smiling when he said it. I wasn't smiling. "Don't you see?" he asked. "All that stuff will turn into water and pour into the Atlantic and Pacific. Ocean currents will change and this means rainfall patterns will change. The Mid-west States will become as drought-ridden as they were in the 1930s."

This was distressing news. I considered the dreadful consequences of such a climatic change. Droughts would cause world-wide crops failures. Hunger would stalk the entire earth. What grim tragedies would surely follow? Aloud I exclaimed "Millions of people will starve to death."

The Major smiled and vigorously nodded his head. "Yes," he agreed, "you are correct. Starvation will kill millions. All by itself, global warming can solve the world's terrible over-population problem, but that's not the only advantage of the melt down. Ocean levels will rise dramatically. San Francisco and Los Angeles will be submerged. So will the east coast." Peabody smiled broadly as he contemplated such a disaster.

It was obvious these terrifying prospects didn't bother Peabody. He seemed to revel in them. I was stunned by his reaction. For my part, global warming represented catastrophe. World-wide starvation was not my only concern. The floods would destroy Philadelphia. The societal effects would be terrible. Philadelphians would leave the city for higher ground. My clientele would scatter. My practice would be ruined.

I interrupted Peabody, planning to state my displeasure at his apparently gleeful forecasts of drought and the submerging of large cities. "I know you think there are too many people in the world and I know you've always wanted the West Coast to slide into the Pacific," I began. I didn't get a chance to finish my thought. Peabody interrupted my interruption.

"Yes, yes," he said, "but consider the even more pleasing and significant effect of global warming," With drought in the Mid-west, there will be no water for migrating ducks. They will have to abandon their Central fly way." The Major's smile brightened his entire face and, emphasizing each word, he said: "They will move east. There will be more ducks migrating down the Atlantic fly way.

"The rising water will force people to abandon the cities on the east coast," he continued. "Factories will rust away. Cities and their terrible slums will disappear beneath the rising waters. So will millions of automobiles and, as a result, so will our dependence on foreign oil. The submergence of big population centers means smoke and smog will no longer fill the air and none of the cities' offensive effluvia will pump into the air, the lakes and the oceans. Wild rice and duck potato will reappear in profusion. The new eastern shoreline will become a prime habitat for ducks. The hunting will be excellent. Just think of it."

I was thinking of it. I was preoccupied with thoughts of inescapable doom. The future looked grim and I could find no way to alleviate my sense of foreboding. As I predicted, it turned out to be a miserable evening. Major Peabody, however, was in a jovial mood.

I found it impossible to enjoy a dinner. I cancelled the reservation, made my excuses and left as quickly as I could. I was enveloped in clouds of gloom and dismal ruination. The four horsemen of the apocalypse - Pestilence, War, Famine and Death - filled my thoughts as I drove back to my apartment

I was miserable. I was despondent. I was dejected. I was in desperate need of cheering up.

A Snug Man with a Buck

"As you wander through life", said Major Nathaniel Peabody, "if you are not careful - or even if you are - you will meet some very peculiar people. One of them is Karl Adams." Karl is a hunter. He is also a tax accountant. He is the Major's tax accountant and he is reported to be a very good tax accountant. If there is a defensible income tax write off or deduction lurking in an obscure regulation hidden within some incomprehensible provision of the Tax Code, Karl is sure to uncover it.

The Major and his accountant are, in this regard, in perfect agreement. The Major is congenitally ill-disposed toward any government, in general, and to all forms of taxation in particular. Karl's originality and inventive imagination in tax calculations is one of the reasons Major Peabody uses his services.

Because many hunters are numbered among his clientele, when Karl prepares his own tax return, he writes off not only the cost of his various hunting trips, but also the costs of buying, training, feeding and providing veterinarian costs for his German Wirehair retriever, John D. Rockefeller (called "Rocky"). Karl is convinced they are all legitimate business development expenses.

Karl Adams hates to be a part of any unnecessary departure of funds from his clients' bank accounts, especially if they go to the Internal Revenue Service. That hatred turns into an uncontrollable rage when it comes to his own bank account. As far as the accountant's own funds are concerned, that uncontrollable rage and detestation is not limited to sending money to the governmental. Sending it anywhere is a painful operation.

Though Karl has a thriving practice and is far from being destitute, he is certainly not ostentatious concerning his substantial personal wealth. When the sun is down and the hunters have eaten and tended to the care of their weapons and dogs, the gang is apt to leave camp and visit the nearest town for a bit of R and R.

As soon as the Christian Science Reading Room is closed, Peabody tells me, the men usually wander off to the nearest saloon. There, he informs me, people customarily buy libations for other people, back and forth, and forth and back, and so on.

"During such moments of conviviality," Major Peabody reports, "I've had many opportunities to carefully watch my accountant's participations in the sociable activity. In spite of his ample financial reserves, when it comes his time to buy, you wouldn't think he had a penny to his name."

Stories of his reluctance to separate himself from the coin of the realm are legion. Peabody told me the accountant wears his prescription glasses only when he is reading or looking at figures. It is rumored he limits his use of them because he doesn't want to wear them out prematurely.

According to the Major, the ten dollar bill Karl lost during last year's grouse camp poker game bore the signature of the lady who was Treasurer of the United States during the Harry Truman administration. Karl claimed it had been in his family for three generations and was a valued heirloom. This, he says, was the reason for the tears he so copiously shed when he was forced to part with it.

Karl married on December 25th. Some say he had an over-whelming (and obviously transitory) impulse to commemorate the religious holiday. Others believe he was motivated by the fact of getting his wife as an income tax exemption for the entire year. According to Major Peabody, there was an additional reason for the Christmas Day nuptials. Karl was able to get a way with a single gift for both a wedding anniversary and a Christmas present.

I believe you've captured the message. Karl Adams is a snug man with a buck. .

In addition to the careful attention he gives to the management of his assets, Karl has his cholesterol checked periodically and jogs. The Major believe none of these activities does any permanent damage to him.

Commenting on the health aspect of Karl's life, Major Peabody says: "If the media or the medicos create a new disease, Karl immediately makes a list of the reported symptoms. If he feels he has one or more of them and the feeling persists for more than twenty-four hours, he faces a terrible dilemma.

"Trips to the doctor's office, you will recall, are not free. When Karl develops 'symptoms', a pattern emerges. First, he considers the potential cost, then he becomes depressed, and, finally, he decides to visit the medico. I can report, without hesitation, mental reservation or secret evasion of mind whatever, he has never enjoyed paying a medical bill."

Karl and Rocky spend a lot of time in the woods and they are not strangers to wood ticks. You can imagine the accountant's agony when Lyme's disease became popular. It was possible to have the disease and have no specific symptoms. That didn't seem fair to Karl. At the very least a man should have some sort of physical discomfort to justify giving money to a doctor.

Last winter, Rocky began to act sickly and Karl suspected Lyme's. Being a prudent man, he called the animal doctor for a quote. Doc Fischer informed him the standard charge for such a test was twenty five dollars. Since the people doctors told him they charged fifty dollars, Karl thought the vet's price was right.

When he asked Doc Fisher: "How much for two", the vet immediately became suspicious. He knew Karl was tighter than the credit manager at Moskin's used clothing store. He suspected Karl would bring his friends' dogs to the clinic if he gave him a simple cheaper-by-the-dozen quote. So he answered: "The second test gets a fifty percent discount, but you can't bring any dogs you don't personally own."

The vet knew Karl owned only one dog, Rocky. He thought he had outsmarted the accountant. Well, he was wrong. Karl appeared with Rocky and demanded two tests - one for the dog and one for himself. Doc Fischer had to keep up his side of the bargain.

In the end, the vet got the best of Karl.

Doc Fisher added a note to the Report when it came back from the laboratory showing neither blood samples showed signs of Lyme's disease, The note said: 'The dog named Karl has incipient Distemper and should receive immediate attention before it progresses to an uncontrollable state'.

Karl had to pay Doc Fischer eighty dollars to get four distemper shots."

Carpenter Ants

It was October. Paul Cowdery, a Minneapolis attorney, learned of large numbers of illegal migrants planning to surreptitiously cross the Canadian border and settle in and around the hunting property he owned in northern Minnesota. He asked Major Nathaniel Peabody and Doc Carmichael to help him and two friends defend his property from the invasion of the undocumented woodcock reportedly in the process of coming south from Manitoba.

The first evening found the five men seated around the cabin poker table. "Your deal, Counselor," said Major Peabody, a bit glumly. His enthusiasm was limited because no woodcock were found during either the morning or the afternoon hunt. It was also limited because the poker game was approaching its end and he was over forty dollars beneath ground zero.

The lawyer finished scooping up the pot, gathered the cards and began to shuffle the deck, very slowly. He enjoyed shuffling slowly when Peabody was behind. He knew the Major would be anxious to get a new hand and a new opportunity to recover losses. The slow shuffle would irritate him and perhaps interfere with his concentration.

"Five Card Stud," the attorney announced as he began to give each player a face down card. Then he paused, just before giving one to the Major. He looked at him and inquired: "Peabody, do you know what's good for Carpenter ants?" He quickly amended his question. "I mean, do you know what's bad for them. I don't want to encourage them. I want to kill them." The Major answered the question with two words. "Deal, Counselor."

"Carpenter ants?" Jeff Campbell repeated.   Jeff was a dentist. He couldn't shoot worth a tinker's dam, but he was a popular member of the hunting group. He was an accomplished camp cook. "They're destructive little creatures, if I recall correctly."

The lawyer gave out a few cards and, after a quick glance at the Major for signs of annoyance, he stopped, placed the deck on the table and said: "The word 'destructive' doesn't begin to describe them."

Doc Carmichael got into the act with: "Carpenter ants have digestive tracts that can handle cellulose. They eat a lot of wood. They're like termites, but termites don't come this far north."

"Deal," Peabody muttered. The slow deal continued, again stopping just before the Major got his second card.

"Well," the lawyer said to no one in particular, "I've found some of them here in the cabin. I scatter Diazinon crystals outside the place, but the Carpenter ants keep coming back. It's downright discouraging."

"They'll destroy your cabin if you don't attend to them," Doc Carmichael's warned. He peeked at his hole card after getting a Queen face up. (*"If he had a Queen in the hole, he probably would have remembered it,"* Peabody thought.) Out loud he said: "Deal," and the lawyer continued distributing the cards - very slowly.

The Major was well aware of the lawyer's ploy. He knew the slow dealing was meant to throw him off his game. It succeeded in irritating him. Oh, how he wanted revenge. He prayed the Poker Gods would give him the opportunity to make the attorney pay for his impertinence, but this was not the hand.

The fifth man at the table was Dudley Huff. He was a local timber man and knew the woods. More importantly, he knew where grouse and woodcock were apt to be. "That's the trouble with Diazinon," he said. "It wears out. What you need is chlordane. It'll last forever. Spray some of it around and if an ant crawls over it five years from now, he's a dead ant." He looked at his cards. "I believe my Ace is worth fifty cents".

Carmichael followed and Peabody folded. Jeff mucked his cards, saying: "The trouble with chlordane is its long life. It doesn't degrade and people claim it will give you cancer. The government won't allow you to use it for Carpenter ants, but, I'm told, they've made an exception in the case of termites." The attorney, Peabody noticed, paid attention to the Diazinon/chlordane chatter. Without bothering to look at his hole card, the attorney absently added a chip to the pot.

"Sounds like a typical government operation," Peabody said. "They'll allow you to die of cancer if you have termites, but won't allow you to die of it if you have Carpenter ants. When I was a lad in Virginia, it was before the Age of Chemicals. We didn't have chlordane, but we certainly did have termites. We had a natural method for terminally discouraging them. I understand it was used back in pre Civil-War days when the land was a working plantation. I'm quite sure the method was brought over from Africa."

The Major succeeded in capturing the attorney's attention. Diazinon didn't work to the lawyer's satisfaction. Chlordane would, but its use was both illegal and dangerous to the health. If there were a legal, safe and environmentally friendly way to permanently polish off the Carpenter ants, now busily engaged in eating his cabin, Cowdery meant to discover it. Major Peabody, he thought, might know of such a method. He dealt at a normal pace, paying little attention to either the cards or to the betting.

As he distributed the fourth cards, his eyes and thoughts were focused on the Major. Carmichael showed a Queen and little else. Dudley had an Ace. The lawyer showed a pair of tens, but, apparently, he wasn't aware of it. Dudley bet his Ace, Carmichael raised and the lawyer contributed more chips to the growing pot. He was preoccupied with Peabody's termite killing information and looking forward to ridding his cabin of the threat from the Carpenter ants.

"You say you had a way of killing termites?"

"We did, indeed."

"For good?"

"Yes, it was a very successful way of wiping them out." Peabody rattled his ice cubes. The lawyer laid the deck on the table and began to reach for the Major's glass, intending to re-fill it himself. Jeff beat him to the punch and Peabody continued his termite talk.

"Years later," he said, "when I was hunting in Africa, I found the natives using a similar, if not the same, system. They eradicated whole colonies of termites. And you know how many termites there are in Africa. Huge, ugly stalagmites full of them."

"Do you think the system could kill Carpenter ants?"

"There's no reason why it shouldn't. I'm sure it would be just as effective as it is with termites."

During the conversation, the attorney automatically dropped chips into the pot. When the final call was made, he looked at his hand for the first time. He dropped. He didn't have enough to compete in the face of a bet and a raise. Doc Carmichael did have a hole card Queen. His ladies carried the day. The attorney didn't seem to mind.

Peabody gave no indication of volunteering to divulge his secret. *Perhaps,* the lawyer thought, *I might give him a little nudge.* "Major", he said, as he passed the deck to Carmichael, "I'd give fifty dollars to learn how they killed termites."

"I'm sure I can dig it up somewhere, Counselor. I'll send it to you together with all necessary instructions as soon as I get back to Philadelphia. And," he added, pointedly, "it will not be occasioned by the delays some of us experience while waiting for the cards to be dealt."

* * * * *

Back in Philadelphia, Major Peabody chuckled as he considered the Minnesota hunt. The lawyer's fifty dollars covered his poker losses. True to his word, the Major allowed no delay in sending him the guaranteed ant killer program. He addressed and packaged the small parcel after adding the promised instructions:

Place Carpenter ant on Block A.

Place Block B on top of Carpenter ant.

Squeeze blocks together.

All About Loons

Doctor Carmichael invited Major Nathaniel Peabody to join him and a group of Philadelphia hunters on a five day quail hunt at a posh game farm in southern Georgia.

Unfortunately, the hunt was scheduled for the twenty-third to the twenty eighth day of the month. Unfortunately, Major Peabody, in his usual profligate manner, had managed to spend practically all of his monthly income and didn't have the money needed to fund the expedition. Tragically (from his point of view) he had been unable to convince me to give him an advance payment from the Peabody Spendthrift Trust.

Doctor Carmichael was well aware of Major Peabody's love of Georgia quail hunting. The Doctor and Peabody were good friends, but that didn't stop either one from tormenting the other. As soon as he returned to Philadelphia, Carmichael immediately visited Peabody.

In detail, he reported the comfort of the game farm's lodging, the competence of its staff, the excellence of its culinary facilities, the perfection of the dogs and the quality of the substantial quail population. He punctuated his narrative with phrases like: "Too bad you weren't there, Major," "You would have enjoyed it, Major," "You missed the best quail hunt of the century, Major" and "Sorry you couldn't make it, Major."

At Carmichael's hands, Peabody suffered through a 21st century version of the tortures of the Spanish Inquisition. The Major's reaction to losing an opportunity to participate in a great hunt can be imagined only by those who understand his obsession with bird hunting. Peabody's other reactions, however, could easily be predicted. He didn't blame himself for his own incorrigible lack of financial prudence. He blamed me and displayed his ire on the following day - the last day of the month.

During the dinner at Bookbinders - the one I customarily provide on the evening before the delivery of his Trust fund remittance - Major Peabody's conversation dealt with subjects calculated to disturb me. He told tales of vicious bears, poisonous snow snakes, man eating wolves, quill throwing porcupines, scorpions and venomous spiders. He succeeded in scaring the hell out of me. Now, as I tried to enjoy a libation in his apartment while awaiting the stroke of midnight, he began castigating both me and my profession.

After a discourse intended to convince me Jack the Ripper was a 19th century London trust attorney, the Major rattled the ice cubes in his empty glass. It was his unspoken order for another of the same. As I walked to the kitchen to prepare a re-fill, the Major informed my retreating back: "I believe the Bible warns trust attorneys never to tell the truth, claiming that if they do so just once, people will expect them to do it again."

I did my best to hide it, but I was annoyed and irritated. I did not look forward to the next two hours. I knew Peabody would spend every second of it attacking me. Then I noticed a pamphlet on the Major's breakfast table. It was entitled All About Loons. It contained information collected by the Sigurd Olson Environmental Institute at Northland College and was printed by the Endangered Resources Fund as its Publication # ER-006 85. Apparently, Peabody had embarked on a study of Loons.

I felt like a man, drowning in the ocean, who suddenly discovers a lifeline being thrown from an approaching Coast

Guard Cutter. If Loons were Peabody's current enthusiasm, it should be easy to shift the subject matter of his conversation from denigration of the legal profession to rhapsodizing about the Common Loon.

Here was an opportunity to change the subject. I could take his mind off quail and his missed opportunity as well as his immediate obsession with castigating me. As I mixed another brace of single malt Scotch and waters I perused the pamphlet and, with lifted spirits, returned to the living room.

"I see you have been studying the Loon," I said, handing him both the publication and his refreshed libation. "Fascinating bird, the Common Loon," I continued. "This pamphlet says it has developed a vocabulary. It wails when it becomes separated from its chicks or calls for its mate. It hoots to show curiosity. It yodels to show aggression and it uses a tremolo call when it has been disturbed. Amazing! Don't you think that's remarkable?"

"There is some interesting information contained in the publication," Peabody admitted as he picked up the document. "However, it raises more questions than it answers." The Major reached for his glasses and opened the pamphlet. "For example, here on the second page we are told: 'Both air and land pollution has decreased the Loon's chance for survival.'

"That fact, by itself, should come as no surprise, but on the third page we are informed: 'It is impossible to determine the sex of a Loon without observing its internal organs'. This is fascinating information. Of course, it should concern everyone who is interested in the well-being of the Common Loon. It also causes one to wonder about the accuracy of the pamphlet.

"If Loon gender can be determined only after observing its internal organs, you can imagine the problems confronting the birds during their mating season. If, as you point out, the Sigurd Olson Environmental Institute study proves the Loon is capable of vocabulary, ask yourself this question: Wouldn't the first words learned by the Loon be: Sorry, I thought you were a female, or: Hey. Just what the hell do you think you're doing?"

Hurrah! I was off the hook. Peabody had taken the bait. His conversation would now be "Loon directed". No more slanderous attacks upon me for the rest of the evening. All I had to do was make an occasional encouraging sound and the Major would talk about the Common Loon until the stroke of twelve. I could relax.

"What a cogent commentary," I said.

"I have no interest in throwing stones at the good work of the people of the Endangered Species Fund," the Major explained, leaning back in his chair. "However, the accuracy of the All About Loons pamphlet is doubtful. The people who prepared it might find a bit of constructive criticism to be helpful.

"If the Fund wants to protect the Common Loon from extinction, they shouldn't bother with publishing a short pamphlet purporting to tell All About Loons. They should dedicate all of their resources to discovering how to easily tell the sex of a Loon without having to cut it open. Educating the Loons with an easy way to tell the sex of those sharing its species would, undoubtedly, result in a Loon population explosion. The bird would soon be saved from any possibility of being considered an Endangered Species."

"I never thought of it that way. I believe you're right," I said, encouraging him to continue. And Peabody continued.

"This Loon publication," the Major said, "tells us there are four different species of Loons in the northern hemisphere. The Arctic Loon, the Red Throated Loon and the Yellow Billed Loon stay in Canada and Alaska the year around. The Common Loon is more venturesome, but, according to this pamphlet, it will travel no further south than Minnesota, Michigan and

Wisconsin. I find that claim to be preposterous."

"How very interesting", I said, trying to look very interested.

"If Loons venture no further south than those three mid-western states, how can you explain the presence of the 535 Loons inhabiting the Senate and the House of Representatives in Washington D.C.?

"Frankly," Peabody added, "I find fault with the Fund's selection of the title for their pamphlet. 'All About Loons' is a manifest misnomer. The Fund's report doesn't even mention that more primitive and particularly vicious species of Loon who have developed the ability to draft Spendthrift Trusts. Let me tell you about them."

I had spoken too soon. I should have known better. Sadly, I resigned myself to another few hours of castigation.

The Dog Whisperer

You must excuse a dog's shortcomings.
After all, he's only human.
- C. J. Wuss

Major Nathaniel Peabody answered the doorbell, thinking (or, perhaps, hoping) it might be his attorney arriving unannounced to invite him to dinner at Bookbinders. However, it was Albert Wilson Meeker, the Third and it surprised him. Albert Wilson Meeker III was the one man the Major would never expect to ring his doorbell.

It was nearly five years since Major Peabody first hunted with Albert Wilson Meeker III. He never hunted with him again. The Major is capable of overlooking modest personality deficiencies in any man who invites him to a hunt. Meeker's defects of character, however, fell into the "glaring personality deficiencies" category. Moreover, the man had not the slightest suspicion he embodied deficiencies of any kind whatsoever.

Vain, indulgent, self centered and insensitive, Albert Wilson Meeker III believed everyone shared the opinion of the high esteem which he assigned to himself. Major Peabody did not like him. Dogs did not like him. The men who hunted with him only grudgingly put up with him. Behind his back they called him "The Third". Actually, that was not the nickname they called him. It sounded a lot like "Third", but it used only four of the five letters. In fact, it was a word with an Elizabethan origin.

"Hello, Nathaniel," Meeker said as he pushed past the

Major and, uninvited, entered the apartment. "It's been a few years, but I still remember the great time we had in South Dakota." Peabody remembered the time (he couldn't forget it), but he had no recollection of it being great. Meeker went directly to the Major's favorite wing backed chair and sat. "Sit down," he ordered the still standing Major. "I want to talk to you."

Peabody obediently sat. "I'd offer you a drink, Albert," he said, "but I just ran out of Scotch." Then he compounded that lie by adding: "I don't have much time. I've got an appointment with my attorney in another half hour. Complicated tax matters that need…."

"I want to talk to you about my dog," Meeker interrupted, apparently not hearing a word of the Major's attempt to get rid of him.

"Oh?" said Peabody.

"Yes. I'm having a bit of difficulty with him. I understand you have some kind of rapport with dogs so I decided to take advantage of your expertise."

"Oh?"

"Pinky is my German Shorthair and I paid plenty of bucks for him - a lot more than you'd be able to afford. The breeder assured me Pinky came from a long line of exceptional bird dogs - Blue Ribbon field trial stuff, he told me. Great instincts bred into the animal, he guaranteed. Well, I shipped Pinky off to a trainer who came well recommended. I was sure he knew what he was doing when I saw the size of his bill. Only a really skilled dog trainer could get away with charging that much."

Peabody made a show of looking at his wrist watch, raising his eyebrows and exclaiming. "I didn't know it was this late. I've really got to get…"

"You won't believe this, Major," Meeker interrupted. "I immediately had trouble with Pinky. He didn't want to leave the trainer's kennel. He cowered when I repeatedly yelled at him to 'come'. I had to grab his leash and jerk him out of there. I took him hunting and he behaved abominably. He'd work in front of the other hunters, but he wouldn't work anywhere near me. I cuffed him a few times. It didn't help much."

"I can't understand why a good cuffing didn't produce results," Peabody muttered.

"I agree, Major," Meeker said, oblivious to Peabody's sarcasm. "It certainly didn't have the affect I expected. Pinky hunted in front of me during the afternoon, but the birds he flushed were well beyond shotgun range. The men I hunted with gave Pinky doggie treats, patted him on the head and kept saying 'good dog'. I know they were trying to be helpful, but it didn't do any good. Pinky would hunt for them, but he wouldn't hunt for me."

Meeker didn't notice the Major close his eyes and slowly shake his head in disbelief of the man's inability to understand his hunting companions' approval of Pinky's antipathy toward him. "That dog trainer did a rotten job," Meeker grumbled. "I took the dog back to him and complained."

"And?"

"The trainer called me the next morning. Can you imagine the nerve of the rascal? He claimed there was nothing wrong with the dog. While driving home, I saw a worrisome change in Pinky's behavior. Whenever I get close to him, he'd growl at me. When I tried to cuff him, he snapped at me. He nipped a hole in my sleeve. It was a very expensive English tweed jacket."

"Whatever would motivate Pinky to growl at you?" the Major asked. "Surely, your considerate treatment of the animal should have made Pinky admire and respect you."

"I agree, I agree," Meeker agreed, "but there you have it. Pinky attacked me for no good reason. I'd like you to take him for a few weeks and see if you can rehabilitate him. I won't insult you by offering to pay for your services."

The outline of a plan began to form in Peabody's mind. "It sounds like you've got a vicious animal on your hands, Meeker," he announced. "I'm not sure anything can be done. Who named him Pinky?"

"I did," Meeker admitted.

The Major's response was: "Hmmnnn". He slowly nodded his head, paused for a few seconds of contemplation and then asked: "Did you have Pinky fixed?"

"Of course," Meeker answered.

"Hmmnnn. You have a very serious problem, Meeker."

"How serious?"

"The dog is planning to kill you."

"WHAT?"

"Yes, Meeker. Pinky intends to murder you. You're lucky you got home with no more damage than a torn jacket." Meeker's jaw dropped, his eyes opened widely and his eyebrows rose to their maximum height as he telegraphed his consternation. "To those of us who are experienced in dog psychology," the Major continued, "it is obvious. To give a hunting dog a name like 'Pinky' can destroy its self-image. Think of how the other dogs - 'Hunter' or 'Bruno' or 'Max'- would kid a hunting dog named 'Pinky'. Add your decision to neuter him and you can understand why the dog hates you.

"Apparently, Pinky is rebelling as a result of the humiliation suffered because of his name and the degradation caused by the neutering. Clearly, he believes only one kind of revenge will salvage his honor. Yes, Meeker, Pinky will be satisfied only when he has killed you."

"Good God, Peabody. You're right," Meeker exclaimed as he leaped from the chair. "That damned dog is out to get me. I'll have the vet put him down immediately."

"No need to run the risk of getting that close to Pinky," Peabody said, putting his arm around Meeker and gently leading him toward the door. "I'll pick him up tomorrow morning and, one way or another, I'll get rid of him for you."

Meeker was relieved. "You are, indeed, a good friend, Major," he said. "Some day we'll have to go back to South Dakota for another of those great hunts."

Peabody's response was: "Ahhh.... yes ....ahhh ....well .. ..ahhh.... I'll check my schedule."

* * * * *

Doc Carmichael was still in his hunting clothes when he dialed the Major's telephone number. "Hello, Peabody," he said. "Pinky and I just got back from the game farm. He is a jewel. Of course, I thought you were trying to peddle a dog that couldn't hunt or one with a bad nose, but I apologize for thinking you had something up your sleeve. I can't remember when I've worked with a better bird dog.

"Before you change your mind, you've got a deal," Carmichael quickly added. "I'll be over this afternoon with the $600. Frankly, I wonder why you'd ask so little for such a great dog."

"Assign it to the large volume of the milk of human kindness that runs through my veins," the Major explained. "I felt sorry for the poor animal. I suspected Pinky was an excellent hunter. I knew his owner was a jerk and I knew the dog was being abused. I wanted to find a good home for him."

Peabody didn't tell Carmichael the $600 just happened to be the amount he needed to finance a pheasant hunt in Iowa.

Don't Foot Around with Major Peabody

The lovely Stephanie invited me to escort her to the tenth annual reunion of her so-very-exclusive finishing school. I had attended the fifth annual reunion. It was an experience I shall never forget. I did not fit in with the rest of the celebrants. When introduced to them, I was rudely cross-examined. One of the lovely Stephanie's college friends, named Linda something or other, questioned my lineage and found me to be socially unacceptable. The word immediately passed throughout the entire assemblage.

"His great-great-grand parents came over from Germany in 1843? Oh dear." she whispered to a friend and quickly walked away, leaving the impression I was carrying the Black Plague. Later she was heard to say: "Poor Stephanie. He's practically an immigrant. How can she let herself be seen with him?" I decided I would never, never ever attend another of those ghastly affairs.

I enjoy being in the presence of the lovely Stephanie. Nevertheless, when she asked me to escort her to that reunion, I had to find a way to decline. The prospect of a luncheon, a soiree and a dinner followed by a country club dance - all in the presence of her finishing school sisters and their thin blooded husbands - was terrifying.

I immediately recalled a non-existent client and a non-existent case and a non-existent trial. I would be tied up for at least two days. The trial, I ruefully reported to her, was scheduled to begin on the same day as her class reunion. To be on the safe side, I told the trial would be held in Utah.

I was pleased with the deception. I complimented myself by thinking it was the sort of story Major Peabody would fabricate. The lovely Stephanie bought it. But, 'Oh what a tangled net we weave when first we practice to deceive.' The lovely Stephanie asked for the name of the senior member of my firm. She planned to call him, introduce herself, explain her problem and demand he send some junior partner to Utah to handle the case.

When she reached for the phone, I panicked. My association with the Smythe, Hauser, Engels and Tauchen law firm could easily come to an abrupt ending. I could imagine the reaction of the humorless Roberson Smythe when a strange young lady demanded he send a lawyer to replace me in the defense of a bogus client at a bogus trial in a far away State - and all because of a conflict with her social calendar. Heads would roll. At least, one particular head would roll.

I asked myself what the Major would do if he found himself in such a pickle. The answer was immediate. He would find some way to insinuate me into the equation and let me struggle with the problem. Perhaps I could do the same for him.

I reminded the lovely Stephanie of the very minor and insignificant incident with "friend" Linda who felt my family had not been on the continent for an appropriate amount of time. I reported the acute pain I would feel if Linda, inadvertently, of course, caused the lovely Stephanie any discomfort because of my presence. I told her Major Peabody was a direct descendent of early Virginia settlers who were here in the New World before the Pilgrims landed. Peabody would be an excellent escort. The lovely Stephanie thought the Major would be a marvelous substitution and gave up the idea of calling Robertson Smythe.

I called the Major, lied to him, bullied him and played upon his admiration for the lovely Stephanie. He agreed to be her escort and I was off the hook.

* * * * *

When Linda received the lovely Stephanie's notice of attendance and identification of escort, she checked historical society records and discovered Peabody's Virginia pedigree. She was livid. The Major's colonial credentials were better than hers.   Looking for dirt, she Googled him - and she found it. She uncovered Peabody's extensive hunting activities. Linda convinced some of her anti-gun classmate to put the Major in his place. By painting him as a gun owning, bird murdering monster, she'd teach the lovely Stephanie for attempting to up-stage her by bringing an escort with more solid colonial credentials.

Peabody entered the reception arena and smiled when he saw the white shirted, black tied bartender produce 23 year old single malt Macallan whisky. He brought white wine to the lovely Stephanie, now surrounded by a contingent of classmate and spouses. Stephanie introduced him and wandered off to mingle and socialize.   The assault on the Major began immediately.

"I understand one of your ancestors may have been in Virginia during the early 1600s," the lady ringleader purred. Peabody simple pleaded guilty. "I cannot understand why those people brought firearms with them," she added. One of Linda's friends took up the cudgel. "Yes. It was the start of the gun culture that brought this nation so much misery. All the death and destruction we suffer began with your ancestors." Another confederate jumped in. "If those people had left their guns in England we would have become a non-violent society. We'd still have the beautiful passenger pigeon, the Great Auk and lots of interesting animals and things."

Peabody's expression didn't change. On the surface, at least, he remained placid and restrained, conditions requiring some effort on his part. His thoughts were quite different. *"Now I understand why that sneaky attorney ducked out of this affair and shanghaied me into it. He'll pay for this."*

Linda's husband got into the act. "You kill things, don't you?'

That did it. The Major realized he had been targeted for abuse. He decided to respond in full attack mode. His first reaction was to say: "Yes, and occasionally I get violent," and then poke the man in the nose. He knew the lovely Stephanie wouldn't approve, so he pursued a different course.

"I've always admired that painting of your own Massachusetts Pilgrim fathers. You know, the one showing them walking through the snow to attend church. One of them is carrying a firearm. Did you ever wonder why he carried that long gun? Could it have been for protection?

"One of the men who came over on the Mayflower- a fellow named Nathaniel Morton - was the colony's Clerk. He wrote a book entitled "New England Memoirs". He tells about the first time the Indians attacked the colonists. It was December 8, 1620 - just twenty-seven days after the Mayflower sighted land. Mile Standish and a few others of those Massachusetts Johnny-come-latelys were looking for a place to build Plymouth. If they hadn't been able to run through a shower of arrows, get back to their shallop and retrieve their matchlocks, they all would have been killed."

Linda, her confederates and the others who followed to watch the fun didn't expect this kind of rebuttal Unaccustomed to being challenged, they looked at each other and wondered if they should engage in debate. Before any of his politically correct adversaries could speak, Peabody continued his attack.

"King Philip's War is another interesting event. It occurred some fifty years after your Pilgrim Fathers landed. The French provided the Algonquians with modern flintlock rifles. The colonist militias still fought with matchlocks and pikes. About a third of the English settlers were killed during that two year war. Every English settlement west of Concord was destroyed. It could have been the end of the English in New England.

"As near as I can discover, King Philip's War was the first time we learned of the necessity to maintain an up-to-date well armed and well trained militia. Even today, some people have a hard time understanding a heavy price must be paid if we let our army go to pot. Do you agree?"

No one answered.

Peabody was on a roll. "Of course, you all remember the First Thanksgiving Dinner. Do you think the food was brought over on the Mayflower? Some Pilgrims with matchlock firearms went into the woods and came back with venison and turkeys and ducks. Undoubtedly, they provided many other meals for the Pilgrims. Without firearms the colonists might have starved to death.

"Your ancestors came to a wilderness and created a nation. It couldn't have been done without guns. In 1775, when someone whose genes you now carry stood on a bridge at Concord and faced the British army, he carried the musket that usually hung over the fireplace in his home. History would be different if he carried a stick."

Peabody had said enough. "This certainly is a wonderful reunion," he said, abruptly changing the subject. "It's a pleasure to be with people who provide their guests with fine single malt whiskey." He turned, walked, alone, toward the bar and repeated his promise: That lawyer is going to pay for this.

The Spiney Pig

The dinner at Bookbinders was a strained and quiet affair. Major Nathaniel Peabody was sullen and barely able to disguise his petulance. I knew the reason for his ill-humor. It was the last day of the month and it was a Saturday. As usual, I had refused to give him his Spendthrift Trust remittance until the stroke of midnight. Therefore, Peabody's arrival at the hunting camp in northern Wisconsin was delayed. Therefore, Peabody lost one full day of hunting. Therefore, Peabody directed his displeasure at me. Since he was uncomfortable, he was determined to make sure I, too, was uncomfortable.

At Bookbinders and, later, in the Major's apartment as we awaited the magical time of 12:01 and the delivery of his Spendthrift Trust remittance, Peabody's attitude improved by degrees in direct relationship to the degrees of discomfort he was able to engendered in me.

Major Peabody knows I am a city boy, uncomfortable in the swamps and forests where he and his hunting companions chase ducks and grouse and other dangerous birds and animals. Nevertheless, he insisted on dwelling upon the subjects he suspected would frighten me. His suspicions were correct.

He told a story about a pack of wolves surrounding a lone hunter's evening, wilderness tent. He described the piercing, yellow/green eyes and the blood curdling snarls of the vicious predators as they circled in the edges of the darkness around the man's tent. They waited until the campfire died down before attacking. Peabody took delight in describing the gore and bones the wolves left behind when they had finished their feast.

Then he informed me he would be hunting at the very same spot when I had to deliver his next Spendthrift Trust installment. Not satisfied with the tale of wolf horror, he described other dangers I might encounter when I had to visit his camp. He frightened me with stories of venomous late autumn white snakes, so well camouflaged by October snows that people would unwittingly tread upon them, only to be bitten and die terrible lingering deaths in the cold Wisconsin forests.

He told of hunters who disappeared in the woods near the same cabin, leaving behind nothing more than their hats on the carpet of leaves covering woodland quicksand deposits. Like the La Brea tar pits, the quicksand trapped and slowly dragged its victims down to suffocating death. He told of how he had recovered the body of a fellow hunter by carefully probing into the quicksand with a hay rake, piercing the sunken man's rib cage and hauling him up to the light of day, but too late to save his life.

It was well after eleven o'clock when the Major asked me if I knew anything about porcupines. Of course, he wasn't looking for an educational comment from me. (Doc Carmichael, one of the Major's hunting friends, told me the animal was disagreeable, short tempered and armed with an arsenal of sharp needles. He said it would shoot the needles at me if I ever got close to one of them. I don't know how far the needles will fly, but if I ever encounter a porcupine I will stay at least fifteen feet from it - make that twenty feet from it.)

I answered the Major's question with an entirely truthful statement. "More than I care to know," I said and attempted to direct the conversation in a more pleasant direction by adding, "I'll bet you come across some very interesting wild flowers during your hunts."

"The porcupine is an interesting animal," Peabody responded, "The Spanish call it puerco espino - spiney pig, but it was the French who named it 'porc d'epine'. The word "porcupine" is a direct descendent of the French term." The Major continued to give me unwanted information. "Baby porcupines are called 'porqupets'. Don't you find that interesting?"

No, I didn't find it interesting. My interest in any aspect of the animal was limited - to the point of being non-existent. "Yes. Major,' I answered, "I find it fascinating. Now, about those wild flowers -----.'"

Peabody would not be distracted. "A group of porcupines is called a 'prickle'. A Prickle of Porcupines! What a great expression. The English language is full of such inventive descriptions. A Pod of Whales. A Gaggle of Geese. A Murder of Crows. An Exultation of Larks. More recently, new ones have been coined. An Incompetence of Bureaucrats, a Posturing of Senators and a Thievery of Representatives come to mind.

"They shoot needles at you, don't they?" I questioned.

"Porcupine?" the Major asked. "Oh, yes. Yes indeed. They can be quite painful. Let me tell you about it."

"Wildflowers," I said, showing a touch of panic. "You were going to tell me about the forest flowers you can find in the fall."

"You've met Mike Stoychoff?" the Major asked, completely disregarding my attempt to change the subject. "I don't believe you met his hunting buddy Steve. Well, I was hunting with them when Steve got swatted by a porky. Not swatted," he quickly amended. "The porcupine shot its quills at him - from fifteen or twenty feet, as I recall it. Steve had quills in his head, in his ear, in his cheek - all along the left side of his face.

"A porcupine's quill is built with lots of barbs along its shank, the Major explained. "Like arrowheads, the barbs all point in the same direction. As they dry, the barbs collapse into the shank of the quill. The collapse of the barbs has the effect of moving the quill forward inside a man's flesh. If not removed before they begin to dry, it can be a terribly ugly and nasty business."

Peabody noticed my shudder.

"Yes," he said, "As you can imagine, Steve was in pain and it was going to be more painful. We had to pull the quills out and it was like removing fish hooks by jerking them out backwards."

I shuddered again.

"I tied a rope around Steve's neck and pulled it close to the base of a nearby maple tree. I looped the rope around the tree so tightly that Steve couldn't move his head. Then I lay down on top of him and, while he yelled in agony, Mike pulled the quills out of his head with a pliers."

I was aghast. "Good heavens!" I exclaimed. "The poor man! Did he get proper medical attention? Did he live through it? Was the pliers sterilized? Were there any after effects?"

Before the Major could answer, the clock struck twelve. Peabody extended his hand. I gave him the check and left. I didn't want to hear any more about Steve's encounter with the porcupine. And I didn't look forward to next month's trip to Mike's cabin.

* * * * *

A few weeks later, Mike and Steve were hunting along a creek bottom near Thunder Mountain in Oconto County. In that part of Wisconsin, the Ruffed Grouse cycle was at its nadir. Only two birds had flushed. They were heard, but not seen.

"Well Steve," Mike said, "it's time for us to call it a morning. Let's have lunch and take a snooze. We'll try again this afternoon." The hunters turned and walked back toward Mike's cabin. Steve was in the lead with Mike close behind. Then it happened. Steve saw movement on the ground and immediately recognized a porky, lumbering toward a tree. He ran to it.

Steve had a purpose. He did not like porcupines He intended to grab it by the neck and give it a good shaking. In the past, every time he tried it, the porky had swatted him and won the fight. This time, the dog believed he would surely win.

The Supernatural

Major Peabody sat silently while his hunting companions enjoyed post-dinner libations and discussed the day's hunt. At the moment, Doc Carmichael was under attack because of his hint of the occurrence of a supernatural event.

"Oh, come now," Paul asked him. "You've never been here before. This is the first time you've been in this camp. You don't seriously believe it, do you?

Carmichael was adamant, "It's not a question of whether I believe it or not. I'm only reporting what happened to me. I saw it, and that's the truth. When we drove in and made the turn just before the cabin, I saw that big rock and I knew I had been here before. The scene perfectly matched something I carried in my head. Every tree, every branch, every fern, every dead leaf lying on the ground - I have seen them all before. I even knew the bird was going to fly from behind the fallen spruce."

"Come on, Doc," Paul repeated. "Déjà vu. It's nothing more than your head playing tricks on you. We're not living in the Middle Ages. You should know better."

"Don't be too hard on him, Paul." said Lefty, the other skeptic. "I'm willing to accept the concept of the existence of the supernatural. How else can you explain Doc coming back to camp with two grouse. That's far from a natural happening. He can't shoot that well. That must have been some kind of supernatural event."

Peabody came to Doc Carmichael's defense. "Personally,"

he said as he removed the plastic sheath from his cigar, "I, too, once had difficulty in believing in the supernatural." He lit the cigar, looked at its burning tip and, satisfied, shook the wooden match. When he was sure it was out, he threw it into the wood box beside the stove.

"Everyone has had strange experiences. I am a case in point," he admitted. "In early November, when the Ruffed Grouse season is coming to a close, I am visited by a terrible sense of foreboding. It frightens me. It is an overpowering and almost tangible feeling of approaching doom - as if I were being warned of a disaster about to occur.

"Some would ascribe it to an extra sensory perception, but I was as much of a skeptic as you two," and he waved his cigar in the general direction of Paul and Lefty. "I always thought it was nothing more than my sub-conscious warning me the voters might elect liberals to the House of Representatives, but it might have been something else. Who knows? I told you I once had difficult in believing in the supernatural. Now I am a believer."

"Incredible," Lefty exclaimed. "You mean to say you actually believe in such patent nonsense?"

"I'd rather not talk about it, Lefty, but I think you should not dismiss Doc's thesis out of hand."

"Magic," Lefty said shaking his head in disbelief. "Would you believe it, Paul? The Major and Doc Carmichael believe in magic."

Peabody again studied the glowing end of his cigar. He sipped from his drink. Lefty's sarcasm forced him to respond. He decided to take up the challenge.

"Anyone with friends who have built cabins in the woods has heard stories about driving wells and finding water. Those reports often refer to 'dousers' or to 'water witches' - men and sometimes women who can tell where underground water can be found. I know it is ridiculous. I know it has the powerful aroma of fraud. I don't believe it for a second. But I've seen it happen. I know it works.

"I've seen a douser take a willow switch and walk over open land. I've seen the switch turn down, marking a particular spot. And," the Major added, "I've seen the dowser watch the switch bounce and accurately forecasted the number of feet of pipe to be driven before the water source was reached."

"I guess I've heard of that," Lefty reluctantly admitted.

"Charlie Robbins wouldn't drive a well point without using a water witch," Paul confirmed, and the Major continued his argument.

"We've all sat in a duck blind on bluebird days, watching rafts of duck feed in the center of the lake. They'd be so far out a hunter would need a deer rifle to endanger them. Nothing else could reach them. Then, for no apparent reason and at the same instant, they would all take off. Not a few of them. Not half of them. Every single one of them. Why?

"They don't send notes to one another. One of them doesn't quack 'I think I'll fly away. Anyone want to join me?' They all take to the air at the same time. Is there some force, unknown to us, that orders them to go? Lefty? Paul? You've seen it yourselves, haven't you? Isn't than an example of extra sensory perception? Of the supernatural?"

The Major waited for a response from his doubting friends. Yes, they had seen flocks of duck seemingly moving as a single unit, but could give no rational explanation for the phenomenon. The two hunters looked at each other in confusion and were silent.

Peabody concluded his defense. "At one time, I'm sure Doc Carmichael was just as skeptical as you are. I certainly was. But, if you've ever experienced the supernatural, your skepticism will quickly disappear."

"Then you've experienced it? Paul asked.

"Tell us about it, Lefty insisted.

Peabody again studied his cigar. "I'm reluctant to talk about it. It was, well, it was unbelievable. Suffice it to say, my experience caused me to accept, without question, the presence of supernatural forces." Then he was silent. He rattled the ice cubes in his empty glass. Paul refilled it and Peabody tried to change the subject.

Lefty, Paul and Doc Carmichael would have none of it. They pleaded and cajoled and promised not to laugh or tell anyone about it. The Major finally relented.

"It was in Upper Michigan," he began. "About six years ago. This time of year. We were grouse hunting. I came upon this old woman. She was very old and very wrinkled and had stringy gray hair, but her eyes were bright and lively and dark and somehow penetrating. She was picking fall mushrooms.

"The grouse population was at the bottom of its cycle. The old woman inquired about my luck. I told her I hadn't had a flush, but had seen a nice patch of honey mushrooms. I led her to the spot and, together, it didn't take long to fill both her baskets. I wondered how old she was. I didn't say anything out loud. I just wondered.

"She said: 'I am one hundred years old.' You can imagine my surprise. She had answered an unasked question. Then, with those piercing dark eyes, she looked at me and told me she was a witch. Of course, I didn't believe her. You know how women lie about their age. She looked to be a hundred and five, at least.

"This old woman then said. 'You have been kind and I will help you. You and your 20 ga. Lefever will have good luck.' She turned and disappeared into the forest.

"Gentlemen, I had not seen a bird during the morning and there weren't many birds around. Within an hour I had five

Ruffed Grouse in my game bag."

Lefty and Paul's skepticism returned. They looked at each other with raised eyebrows and conveyed their unspoken agreement: "It's getting pretty deep around here."

"I have a bridge in Brooklyn. Would you like to buy it?"

"But, there's more to it," the Major protested. "She said: 'You and your 20 ga. Lefever will be successful.' Here's the strange part. I've had good luck with my gun, but no one else has been able to hit a thing with it. It's like the gun is lucky for me and cursed for everyone else."

"I'll vouch for that," Doc Carmichael interjected. "I've used Peabody's Lefever a few times and have never killed a bird with it. I don't know how many easy crossing patterns I missed."

"O K," Paul said. "How about a little wager. Say a hundred dollars" Lefty nodded in agreement. "Lefty and I will exchange guns with you and Doc. I'll use the Lefever in the morning and Lefty will use it in the afternoon."

* * * * *

As they drove back to Philadelphia, Major Peabody kept fifty dollars and gave fifty to Doc Carmichael. He thanked him. "You set it up nicely, Doc. I was sure they'd bite."

"What did you use when you reloaded the 20 ga. shells? Sand?" Doc asked.

"No. I used sugar. I though sand might injure the barrels."

Crime and Punishment

On December twentieth, I was helping the lovely Stephanie with her Christmas shopping. That "help" consisted of puppy-dogging behind her as she wandered through posh boutiques and carrying the growing stack of packages containing her purchases. She dawdled in a jewelry store, spent a good deal of time telling me how much she liked a particular diamond broach and then left without buying it or looking at anything else. This seemed like very strange behavior on her part.

The very next day, a clever though occurred to me. I returned to the store, bought the broach and had it wrapped in gold colored paper. I intended to surprise the lovely Stephanie. It was all part of my as yet unannounced brilliant master plan. That brilliant master plan began with a modest end-of-year celebration in Major Nathaniel Peabody's apartment.

My New Year's Eve party had to be held at the Major's apartment because of the provisions of the Peabody Spendthrift Trust. The elder Peabody was painfully aware of his only son's ingenious ability to rid himself of money. The trust document was very carefully and very strictly drawn. Major Peabody's monthly remittance was to be delivered to him on the first day of every month. Any change in terms, early distribution or alienation of any kind were specifically denied.

When the Major first learned he could not tap his trust funds whenever he needed cash, he showed his displeasure by insisting the other terms of the document also be strictly observed - including the one requiring the Trustee (me) to deliver his checks. And that explains why I had to be in Major Peabody's Philadelphia apartment, delivering his monthly Spendthrift Trust stipend when the New Year's Eve clock struck midnight, ushering in not only the New Year, but also the first day of the ensuing month.

The First Stage of my brilliant master plan, therefore, had to be performed within the Philadelphia apartment of Major Nathaniel Peabody, the place where I had to deliver his check. I had already proposed such a New Year's Eve party to the Major and he thought it was a delightful suggestion. On the moment of the arrival of the New Year, I would hand Peabody his check, give the lovely Stephanie her diamond broach and find myself standing beneath the mistletoe, being covered with her warm, moist kisses. Stage Two of my plan consisted of a post-midnight private celebration with the lovely Stephanie in my own apartment. And later, what with the champagne and all, who knows?

Then came disaster.

The lovely Stephanie invited me to escort her to one of the most exclusive New Year's Eve celebrations held in south eastern Pennsylvania. What a disgusting development. I couldn't be her escort. I couldn't be at that snooty Main Line party, standing under the mistletoe with the lovely Stephanie and, at the same time; be in Peabody's apartment delivering his first-of-the-month stipend. I damned the terms of the Peabody Spendthrift Trust. I damned the idiot lawyer who drafted its provisions (me).

In desperation, I reminded the lovely Stephanie of the number of drunks careening wildly up and down the roads and highways. It would be much safer if we celebrated the coming of the New Year in Philadelphia with Major Peabody and, later, perhaps at some other equally safe location. The lovely Stephanie would have none of it. She said "No" in such a firm tone that only a fool would attempt to dissuade her.

I attempted to dissuade her. I told her the ancient Druids celebrated the coming year one week after the winter solstice - which would make it the 29th or 30th of the month. "Wouldn't it be fun if you and your friends decided to celebrated in the old Druid tradition and change the date of their party?" I ventured.

The lovely Stephanie's enthusiasm for my suggestion was limited. Her response was immediate and unqualified. She said "NO !!!!!" She had no intention of spending New Years Eve at a time different from December 31 or at any place other than at that fancy Main Line mansion..

In a flash of inspiration, it occurred to me she might be able to wangle an invitation for our mutual friend, Major Peabody. If he were present at her party, I could slip him his check while I was standing under the mistletoe with the lovely Stephanie. I made the proposal. The lovely Stephanie agreed. Oh, joy. I had solved my problem - I thought.

Ten minutes later the lovely Stephanie called to inform me the Major declined her invitation. Of course, I knew why Peabody wouldn't go to the lovely Stephanie's party. Peabody knew I couldn't escort her to that Main Line party if I had to be in his apartment, delivering the trust check at 12:01 a.m. New Year's morning. He was getting back at me for my many refusals to prepay his monthly remittances.

When I told the lovely Stephanie it was impossible for me at attend her party, the temperature of the telephone I held in my hand dropped by a full ten degrees. A minute passed without a sound coming from it. Then, in a flat voice, the lovely Stephanie slowly informed me of her intention to go to the party without an escort. She hoped I might find a way to meet her there. Then I heard a click.

I was disconsolate. For the next days I struggled with the problem of being in two places at the same time. Finally, I concluded it was an impossibility. I directed my attention to other solutions. I could pay someone to kidnap the lovely Stephanie and release her at the Major's apartment a few minutes before midnight. I could burn down the mansion at the Main Line estate. I could kill Peabody. I recognized possible ethical questions involved with each such alternate proposition and reluctantly rejected them.

On the last day of the year, alone, sulking in my apartment, I was not in a cheerful mood. It was apparent the joys of the approaching New Year celebrations were not going to descend upon me. Then, unexpectedly, the answer to my problems flashed across my mind. I could disregard a cardinal provision of the Spendthrift Trust Agreement and deliver Peabody's remittance before 12:01 of January 1.

Suddenly, all was right in the world. If I got to the Major's apartment by eight o'clock, I could give him his check and leave. I'd be at the Main Line party by nine and at midnight I'd be under the mistletoe with the lovely Stephanie. I put two bottles of champagne in my apartment refrigerator. They would be well chilled when the two of us returned from the Main Line party.

I rang the buzzer at Peabody's apartment at a quarter to eight. The door opened and the Major greeted me. "You're early my boy. I didn't expect you for another four hours. I thought you might be piqued by your unfortunate inability to celebrate with Stephanie and might have decided to spend the pre-midnight period sulking in your apartment."

"As a matter of fact," I interjected, "I had intended to do just that, but my plans have changed. In view of the special occasion, it being a brand new year and all that, we can celebrate early. I'll give you your check right now - but you've got to promise not to tell a soul. Happy New Year, Major" I said and proffered his check. Peabody stepped back without touching it.

"Do you remember the first time we met?" he asked. "It was at the Smythe Hauser Engels & Tauchen law office. I desperately needed cash, but you insisted the terms of the Spendthrift Trust did not allow any kind of pre-payment. You insisted the Spendthrift Trust provisions provided for payment only on the first day of the month and those provisions could not be changed.

"Please keep the check until midnight. If you give it to me before January 1, you will violate the terms of the trust. That violation might be used as a reason to petition the court for a new Trustee. The resulting publicity would be a terrible embarrassment to you as well as to all the other lawyers at your firm." Peabody leaned back in his chair and smiled a wicked smile. "I couldn't bear to see that happen."

"You wouldn't do that, would you?" I asked. It was more of a plea than a question. Peabody merely continued his wicked smile. He had me and he knew it. He was torturing me - enjoying his pay-back time.

* * * * *

The television screen showed a huge, cheek-to-jowl, milling crowd watching the big lighted ball descend on Times Square as the announcer counted backwards "ten, nine, eight ..." Over the sounds of festivity, Major Peabody lifted his glass of champagne, smiled and wished me a happy New Year.

"Happy New Year yourself," I snarled and handed him his check.

Play the Cards You Hold

We were in my apartment. Major Nathaniel Peabody settled himself comfortably into my favorite chair and, without asking, took an H. Upmann from my cigar humidor. It didn't bother me. I don't smoke and the Major knows I don't smoke. He gave me the humidor and the box of H. Upmann cigars for a Christmas present. It was his way of assuring himself of a supply of good cigars whenever he visited me.

It was nearly nine o'clock on a Monday evening. On the following morning Peabody and Doc Carmichael wanted to drive to Maine for a bird hunt. Of course, the Major was flat broke and in desperate need of money to fund the hunt expenses. He spent the previous hour trying to convince me to give him his trust check. He had not been successful.

So - Peabody sat before the television set in my favorite chair, sipping my single malt and smoking up my apartment. He intended to remain there until he got his check and could go to Maine. Don't get me wrong. I usually enjoy the Major's presence. Tonight, however, was an exception. I am a Packer fan. The Monday Night Football game would start in another half hour and the Packer's were playing the Miami Dolphins.

Peabody's aversion to both television and to football was well documented. The last time I attempted to watch a game in his presence, I returned from my kitchen with the Major's refreshed drink to find my television set was turned off. A closer examination showed the electric cord had been cut and the end containing the wall plug had vanished.

As long as Peabody was in my apartment, I would have a difficult time trying to watch a football game.

The Major's ulterior motive was clear enough. He knew my Packer preference. He knew he could keep me from watching the game. His unspoken threat was obvious. If I didn't deliver his check, he would stay in my apartment and keep me from watching the Packers. That prospect did not please me, but I had no intention of surrendering. I planned to stick to my guns.

In no uncertain terms, I told him his check was in the top drawer of my desk and there it would remain resting undisturbed through all of Tuesday until Wednesday, Midnight, Eastern Standard Time. (I separately emphasized each of those last seven words.)

Peabody watched a smoke ring rise in the air and slowly dissipate. "There are times when then Fates appear to conspire against you." he said in an unenthusiastic tone. "There are times when men must face the inevitable and, as Longfellow wrote, fold their tents like the Arabs and as silently steal away."

The quotation surprised me. It sounded like a sign of Peabody's surrender. I was pleased to hear him acknowledge the defeat of his attempt to talk me into an advance trust payment. I was not happy to surmise he intended to make me pay for my victory by staying with me and keeping me from watching the Packer game. I'm sure my expression showed it.

"You seen preoccupied, my boy," the Major observed. "I have no idea why you appear to be ill at ease and I won't pry into your personal affairs, but let me offer a bit of advice. One must accept the cards one has been dealt and play them to the best of one's ability. The Fates have not always been kind to me," he explained. "They have challenged me many times and many times I have lost - but sometimes I have won." He paused and smiled, probably thinking of some past event, before telling his story.

"At about this time last year, I was preparing to go to Maine hunting with Michael Durham on Charlie Ainsworth's land. Charlie's cabin is located in the center of some prime Ruffed Grouse covert. Michael is a trial attorney and, therefore, not entirely trustworthy. Still, he is a popular hunting companion. By that, I mean he has a great grouse dog. It's a German Shorthair named Deuces Tecum. 'Deuces Tecum' is lawyer Latin. It translates into English as 'Bring it with you'. It's a good name for a retriever.

"Most hunting dogs flush grouse and too many of them work too far away from their masters. Deuces Tecum occasionally commits that second crime, but not the first one. Deuces Tecum has the ability to find grouse, point them and, most important, keep them from exploding into the air until Michael, with shotgun at the ready, walks up to him.

"It is Deuces Tecum that makes Michael a successful bird hunter. Michael is a very good shot, but he is very nearsighted. He can read law book all right, but things became quite fuzzy when they are more than twenty feet away. Without a good dog to locate the bird and keep it on the ground, Michael might be able to hear a bird take off, but he would never see it in time to shoot at it.

"It was later in October - this time of year. Michael and I were going to drive to Maine for a grouse hunt. Just like Doc Carmichael and I planned to do tomorrow morning. As I loaded my gear into Michael's van, I noticed Deuces Tecum was not with us. Michael didn't mention the dog during our trip. That bothered me. Had it been a simple matter of a trip to the veterinarian or, perhaps, a visit to a lady German Shorthair in need of company, I was sure Michael would have told me of it.

"I feared Michael's silence signaled a tragedy. Certainly, it would be very difficult for a hunter to talk about putting his dog down. I acknowledged his reluctance to speak of it and made no reference to the animal, but I was disappointed. I shared Michael's sorrow. It had been a joy to hunt over Deuces Tecum.

"Our conversations centered on the beautiful colors of the Maine woods, grouse hunting and old, shared experiences. Michael talked of some of the occasions when he had been on the unfortunate side of wagers with me. He wanted revenge and bet he would drop more birds than I during the next day's hunt. I was in an expansive mood so I disregarded my better judgment and agreed to the wager."

"Disregarded your better judgment? Agreed to the wager?" I asked in disbelief. "Without Deuces Tecum, he couldn't see a bird to shoot at. You couldn't lose. You old rascal. You took advantage of a guileless attorney." The phrase 'guileless attorney' elicited a look of disbelief from the Major. He disregarded my comment and continued with his story.

"When we got to Charlie's cabin, the reason for Michael's bet became clear. Deuces Tecum was tied to the door latch. The note pinned to the door said: "Mike - Here's your dog - well fed and watered. Hope you got the Major to bet with you. I'll be in camp tomorrow night. Charlie'."

"That evening, the deceit and duplicity of my companions hung over me like a dark cloud. My gentle nature, however, was sustained by my knowledge that one must play with the cards one has been dealt and, in the morning, my attitude returned to its normal, pleasant condition. When we arrived at the scene of our hunt, as I let Deuces Tecum out of his cage in the back of the van, I stole the clapper from his bell.

"Usually, Michael knows when Deuces Tecum was rigidly at point because the bell on the dog's collar stopped ringing.

Without a clapper in the dog's bell, Michael never knew where he was and never knew if or where he stopped. Michael was decidedly at a disadvantage."

Peabody rattled the ice cubes in his now empty glass. I dutifully retrieved it and went to the kitchen to prepare a replacement. I also made some cracker and aged cheddar cheese hors d'oeuvres. When I returned to the living room, I was ready to spend the next few hours listening to the Major instead of watching the game.

The room was empty. Peabody was gone. I wondered whatever could have caused him to leave so abruptly and without so much as a fare-thee-well. Then I saw the top drawer of my desk was open. The envelope containing his end-of-month remittance was, like Major Peabody, gone. In its stead, I found a note:

"Your subtle telling of the location of my check allowed me access to the moneys you improperly withheld. As a result, it also allows you to watch the Packer game. Very clever of you. Enjoy the game. You've learned to play the cards you've been dealt."

- Peabody

The Sure Thing

I arrived at the grouse camp in time for the evening meal. It was the last day of the month and Peabody's Spendthrift Trust remittance rested safely in my wallet. I was greeted in an effusively friendly manner by Major Peabody and Doctor Carmichael. The other two men, who, apparently, were local hunters, took the news of my arrival in a calmer fashion.

Peabody and the Doctor solicitously inquired into my health and general well being. Doctor Carmichael invited me to sit in the chair closest to the wood stove. It was a thread bare lumpish overstuffed thing that would have been put out on the curb in any town in America, but it was the best one in the cabin. Peabody handed me a Scotch and water and toasted my safe arrival.

The dinner was excellent. The Major prepared the breast of Ruffed Grouse. Its firm white meat was delicious. Doctor Carmichael opened bottles of a vintage year chateau bottled Merlot and, contrary to the usual custom, my glass was always the first one refilled. The other two hunters - John Somebody and Bob Somebody - were polite to me. In other words, all the warning flags were flying.

Whenever the Major and his friends treat me with this kind of respect, experience has taught me abuse and mistreatment are sure to follow. The preferred treatment they extended to me reeked of conspiracy. Something was up their collective sleeves. Call it paranoia if you wish, but I was immediately suspicious and on guard. I resolved to be particularly cautious.

I intended to avoid whatever outrage they had planned.

It was either Bob or John who filled the wood box with the chunks of aged maple neatly piled near the front door of the cabin. Doctor Carmichael started doing the dishes. He poured a pail of warm water into the sink. The pail had been resting on the top of the wood stove and, now empty, he handed it to either Bob or John and asked him to go to the creek for a re-fill. We would need water for the breakfast dishes. These were the jobs usually assigned to me whenever I found myself in a hunting camp.

Instead of the "Get it yourself" policy I had become accustomed to, Major Peabody brought me a Scotch and water and wondered if I was comfortable. This was too much. It was time for the reason of all this strange behavior to be explained. My eyes narrowed as I took the glass and I made no effort to answer his question.

"All right, Major," I said. "What's up?" Peabody leaned close to me. He whispered: "Doc and I told Bob and John that you were a very wealthy and respected Philadelphia attorney. We asked them to be very nice to you."

This was not a satisfactory explanation for the reason behind their deferential treatment. "And…?" I coldly inquired.

"And," Peabody whispered, "you know how nearly impossible it is to enjoy a poker game when there are only four players."

The truth came out. The ulterior motive behind the Major's pleasantries was disclosed. He wanted more than a fifth player. He wanted someone he could count on to contribute to his financial well-being. He had his sights set on me. This time I would not be victimized.

As I stiffened and started to pull away, Major Peabody took a firm grip on my arm and kept me in the chair. "Now, don't be too hasty, young men," he said in low tones. "I know you have been visited by incredibly bad luck and have regularly had most unfortunate experiences at the poker table. This time," he emphasized, "things will be different."

I am sure the expression on my face telegraphed the firm, unyielding and uncompromisingly negative attitude with which I approached any suggestion of again playing poker with Major Nathaniel Peabody. The Major recognized my expression and before I could say anything, he quickly whispered: "Don't say 'NO' young man. You are about to receive the opportunity of a lifetime. This time you can't miss."

Peabody looked over his shoulder. Doctor Carmichael had John (or Bob) occupied with drying the dishes and Bob (or John) hadn't returned with the water. Satisfied he would not be overheard, Peabody told me: "Bob and John are patsies." He went on to explain how they both loved to play poker, but neither had a grasp on the fundamentals of the game.

"Moreover," he whispered to me, "the two of them, combined, don't have the card sense of a garden slug. They know even less about poker than you do. Compared to them, you have the playing ability of Texas Dolly Brunson."

I was not convinced. I remembered the Major's oft repeated admonition: "Fool me once - shame on you. Fool me twice - shame on me." Peabody had fooled me more than once - many, many more times than once. I had been conned into playing with him and his friends on a various occasions and always with disastrous financial results. My better judgment screamed at me: DON'T DO IT, YOU IDIOT. I violently shook my head - from side to side, not up and down.

The Major did not relax his grip on my still rigid arm. "Listen for just a moment, my young friend," he said. "Doc Carmichael and I are convinced this is such a sure thing that we are willing to cover all of your losses up to and including the amount of fifty dollars. And, who knows," he added, "with these two guys at the table, you might come out a winner." He paused, looked pensive and said, more to himself than to me: "Yes, it is possible. You could come out a winner."

I stopped trying to pull away from him. My arm began to relax. "Is that fifty dollars between the two of you or fifty dollars each," I slowly asked.

"That's fifty dollars each," was the Major's quick reply.

* * * * *

For most of the evening, I was actually ahead. Bob and John were not good poker players. When they got too far behind, it looked like the Major or the Doctor folded what seemed to be better hands and let them take the pot. The last half hour or so, my luck ran out and Doctor Carmichael and Major Peabody were the only winners. I lost a hundred and five dollars. John or Bob lost 65 and the other one lost 80.

When the game was over, Doctor Carmichael looked at his companions and said: "It looks like each of you did better than our attorney friend. He and the Major smiled while John and Bob looked glum. I was happy and chuckled to myself. Things had worked out quite well. After getting the one hundred dollar reimbursement, I had lost only five dollars. That's the best I've ever done. I came very close to being a winner. I returned to Philadelphia without knowing what had happened two hours before I got to the grouse camp.

* * * * *

The four hunters returned to camp in the early afternoon. They cleaned their birds and Peabody promised to cook grouse breasts and wild mushrooms for the evening meal. The two local hunters were told it would impress Peabody's attorney who was scheduled to arrive later in the day.

Once inside the cabin, the men kicked off their boots, relaxed and enjoyed a libation. Major Peabody looked at Bob and John. They seemed a bit pensive. "I feel sorry you two had such bad luck at the poker table," the Major said. "My conscience almost bothers me."

"I feel the same way," Doc Carmichael volunteered. "You fellows had such rotten luck. Second best hands are always costly."

"Yes," Peabody agreed. "It's much better to be dealt a bust hand. You can muck your cards before making a serious investment. I wish we could, somehow, make it up to both of you."

"When does your lawyer get here?" Carmichael asked - right on cue.

"He'll be here in a couple of hours," the Major answered. "Hey, I've got a great idea." He turned to Bob and John. "My lawyer is the worst poker player in the civilized world. To be more accurate, he's the worst poker player in the entire universe. If we could talk him into a game, you boys might recover some of your losses.

The Major's suggestion was not greeted with enthusiasm. "After what happened to me during the last two evenings, Bob answered, "I'm more than just a bit gun-shy about playing poker with you two. I suspect John shares my opinion." John immediately enthusiastically nodded in agreement.

Peabody persisted. "Hear me out, Bob. You and John can't miss. This lawyer is a patsy. He has all the card sense of a garden slug. I'll bet you a hundred dollar you'll come out better than the lawyer." Then Doc Carmichael checked in. "And, John," he added," I'll give you the same bet."

* * * * *

Though John and Bob lost eighty dollars and sixty-five dollars at the poker table, they came out better that the Philadelphia lawyer. He lost a hundred and five dollars. That meant they lost their bets with Peabody and Carmichael plus the eighty and sixty-five they lost at the table. Between the two of them, they lost three hundred and forty-five dollars.

Of the one hundred and five dollars Peabody and Carmichael won from the attorney, they had to reimburse him with a hundred. They made a net of five dollar from him.

All in all, Peabody and Carmichael won three hundred and fifty dollars. Not a bad night's work.

Allergies

Major Peabody looked a bit peaked. I inquired into his state of health and was surprised by his answer. "I suffer from an acute allergic reaction," he told me. "It is particularly debilitating and, at times, I am barely able to withstand the potency of its attacks."

"Good Heavens, Major." I exclaimed. "I had no idea. Have you sought medical attention? What does Doctor Carmichael say."

"On occasion, I've discussed the problem with him. He always tells me to take two aspirin and call him in the morning. It's his way of telling me modern medical science cannot help me. No one can alleviate my affliction. I can do nothing except wait until it subsides. Novembers are particularly trying months and this attack is coming close to doing me in."

"Autumn is bad for allergies," I agreed. "What kind do you have? Is it corn smut? Or Goldenrod? Or some kind of pollen? They're bad this time of year. I certainly hope it isn't dog hair or bird feathers or gun powder."

"Nothing like that," he answered. "Bird hunting gives me my only real relief. It helps me take my mind off what has become my terrible autumnal sickness. Unfortunately, the relief afforded by hunting is only temporary."

This was indeed disturbing, but I still had no idea of just what was causing the Major's discomfort. "Just what is causing your discomfort?" I asked him. As soon as he began to answer, I realized I should not have asked the question.

"I am allergic to BS," he confessed, and I knew I was in for a lecture.

"When it comes time for the citizens of this grand Republic to exercise their sacred franchise and determine the character of their government, the powerful and ubiquitous odor of BS - propagated completely by politicians - fills the air.

Its pungency can be estimated by multiplying the number of candidates seeking office by the total amount of money expended on their behalf, multiplied by the number of their acolytes speaking for them on television programs, multiplied by the number of self-proclaimed television pundits who insist on getting into the act.

"Given the pervasive deceit of office seekers and my virulent allergic reaction to BS, you may be able to appreciate the extent of the agony I experience whenever an election season sneaks up on us. This year it has been particularly bad. I've suffered mightily. Listening to political speeches, commentaries and analyses has made my eyes water to such an extent, at times, it becomes nearly impossible for me to see. Just last week I missed a Ruffed Grouse."

"Of course, politicians will resort to the use of any conceivable amount of BS if they think it will fool the electorate into returning them to Washington and, thus, protect them from their greatest fear - that of having to engage in honest labor.

"Still a few defeated politicians are given government jobs, but only on the condition that they leave the country - ambassadorships, for example.

"Others are made presidents of universities. Such appointments do not unduly harm the students. The quality of the educational system is so poor, even defeated politician can do little to cause additional damage.

"Political con artists who have mastered the ability to adopt a phony look of sincerity and emotionally declaim 'I care' or swear they are going to balance the budget are particularly offensive. They will promise anything. Politician's promises and the truth are sworn enemies.

"I do take a degree of solace from my belief that politicians have no intention of performing on the majority of their promises. One of the greater perils we all face is the possibility these mountebanks may actually try to pass laws in support of the insane positions they have espoused.

"There are a number of politicians whose constituents are mostly city people who have never worn out a pair of boots in their entire lifetime. They believe we will do away with crime and achieve universal peace and find everyone holding hand and singing Kum-ba-ya, if only the Congress would pass strict gun control laws.

A few years ago, some politicians mis-read the polls and tried it. Hunters and people with common sense got together and threw a lot of them out of office. Since then they've been fairly quiet, but they're still out there. We should all give thanks to the NRA."

I raised an eyebrow, when the Major added: "Give thanks to the lobbyists, too." Peabody saw my reaction and I began to interpose an objection. Before I could say 'bribery' the Major stopped me.

"Would a law outlawing lobbyists make Senators and Congressmen honest?" He asked. He didn't expect an answer. "For every man who offers a bribe, there is a politician who will take it. For every politician who demands a bribe, there's a lobbyist who will pay it. Tell me, who is to be blamed for bribery, the one who offers it or the one who takes it." I couldn't answer, but I could see his point. If politicians were honest there would be no bribery.

"Yes, "Peabody repeated, "Give thanks to the lobbyists. If

it weren't for them, who would undertake the monumental task of trying to educate a politician? The man you elected to Congress - what does he know about how the economy operates? I don't mean on some college campus. I mean on Main Street. What does he know about foreign trade? Or foreign policy? Or the world's new communication system? Or national security? Left to his own devices he'd pass legislation even worse that what he passes now. The lobbyists' attempts to educate him often keep him from passing some stupid law.

"Luckily, most legislators are wimps and seldom make decisions all by themselves. (Unless of course, they think it will help them get re-elected.) Once elected, they can look forward to a lifetime of squandering the taxpayer's money. It is nearly impossible to throw them out of office.

"Proven insanity is no cause for failure to secure re-election. Committing some morally reprehensible act - or, rather, being caught committing some morally reprehensible act might be enough to do the job. I saw 'might' because, given enough money and a crafty campaign manager the electorate can be led to approve and applaud their action."

"Oh, come now Major," I objected. "There may be some elements of truth in what you say, but don't you think you are overstating you case just a bit? There are 435 Representatives in Congress and 100 Senators. Surely, they're not all thieves."

The Major became pensive. He stared at his Scotch and water. "Of course, you are correct," he admitted. Not all of them are frauds and demagogues. Perhaps as many as…" he thought for a moment "…perhaps as many as 10 of them - oh give them the benefit of the doubt - perhaps as many as 15 could be accused of being honest."

"Then I presume you are not going to vote come Election Day?" I ventured.

"Of course, I'm going to vote. I would miss it for the

world. I'll vote against the candidates who worry me most. I'll sit up all night watching the election return. When it's all over, for a few days I'll feel like I've given birth to a set of broken dishes. I won't be satisfied with the result, but I'll be glad it's over. Soon, my allergic reaction will disappear."

It Ain't Necessarily So

Major Nathaniel Peabody was in Wisconsin. It was the end of the month and I had to go there. I didn't look forward to the trip. I'm accustomed to indoor plumbing, but I can put up with cabins with outhouses. The Major's grouse camp consisted of a few tents pitched on the bank of a remote stream with neither of the above-mentioned amenities.

Though the hunters used paper cups and paper plates capable of being burned in camp fires, I was told they washed the pots and pans by allowing the hunting dogs to lick them clean. I didn't want to think about it. Moreover, Wisconsin has wood ticks and that means it has Lyme's Disease and Rocky Mountain Fever. Moreover, Wisconsin has mosquitoes and that means Malaria and Yellow Fever and the Nile Disease.

I am convinced there are more deadly germs and viruses in Peabody's grouse camp than there are in an urban hospital. I am convinced the sanitary condition in any of Peabody's hunting camps compare, unfavorably, to the horse dung filled streets of London's nineteenth century Gin Alley. I viewed the trip to Wisconsin with fear and trembling.

When I arrived at the scene, Peabody informed me the hunter's had already dawn straws. He drew for me and picked the long straw. I had won. I would have preferred to allow someone else to have that good luck. The winner's prize consisted of the responsibility of performing bartender service while the Major and his friends sat around the camp fire, telling stories and enjoying a libation, or two, or so.

I also won the right to become camp cook for the evening. I would supervise the cooking of the steaks on the charcoal grill, serving same and, after the meal, burning the used paper ware and cleaning the other pots, pans and utensils. I immediately assumed the duties of my office. The burning charcoal was ready for the steaks. I added the condiments and put them on the grill.

I inquired about the location of the water supply and was informed one of the dogs had knocked over the plastic water container and dumped most of its contents on the ground. I suspect the "dog" may have been one of the hunters who over-imbibed during the previous evening's frolic. I used most of the remaining water to wash all non-paper kitchen items. I thought there might have been some truth to the dog dish licking report.

The Major prefers a splash of water on his Scotch and there wasn't much left in the water jug. I picked up a tin pail, intending to go to the stream to fill it. I would put it on the grill and boil it to get a supply of sterile water for the Major's drink. I saw him at the stream's edge and watched as he filled a plastic cup. He turned and came toward the table where beverages were stored. "Major," I warned, "You shouldn't drink water from the stream. It could contain e-coli bacteria or liver flukes. It could kill you. I saw it on television just last week."

Peabody adopted an unmistakable look of disapproval. "I'll bet you once bought a kit to measure the level of radon in your apartment." he said as he poured a bit of water into a second cup and added a generous amount of single malt. Then he added Scotch to the other cup of unsanitary water and handed it to me. I immediately set it on the table and moved a step away from it.

"How did you guess?" I wondered.

"I'm psychic." he answered. "My sixth sense also tells me you gave up beef during the Mad Cow Disease scare."

"Who told you? It must have been the lovely Stephanie."

Peabody ignored me. "It is my considered opinion," he said after tasting and approving his drink, "that the amazing ability of the uncritical public to delude itself is older than dirt. Throughout the ages, the genus Homo sapiens has developed and maintained a marked predilection to believe the un-believable.

"I can recall when bearded crackpots marched up and down the streets proclaiming the gods had finally had enough of us and intended to wipe us out. They carried sandwich board signs demanding we all repent in a timely fashion because the world was coming to an end. Thousand of people, previously suspected of being rational, believed them. Those folks are downright disappointed when the sun and moon stubbornly continue their celestial revolutions without missing a beat.

"Now global warning will polish us off. A few decades ago, global cooling was going to do the job. All Madison Avenue has to do is hang a stethoscope around the neck of some white coat clothed actor. Once done, any product he hawks is automatically presumed to be not only effective for a joyous sex life, but absolutely essential. If anyone with any sort of ridiculous nostrum promises to make you lose weight or scares the hell out of you by reporting some largely imaginary infectious disease, he can sell anything - including peach pits."

I wasn't convinced. "Science," I argued, "has transformed the world. When you first traveled to South America, I'll bet you had to be vaccinated against smallpox, typhoid, para-typhoid, typhus, yellow fever and malaria before you could get a visa." Peabody sipped and nodded.

"In your lifetime, Medical researchers have reduced those hazards to the point where inoculations are seldom required in this hemisphere. The scientific community has a good track record and you should heed its warnings."

Major Peabody pretended he didn't hear me. "The most advanced scientific minds of the Dark Ages," he said, "were convinced they could turn the baser metals into gold. They spend a lot of time searching for the Philosopher's Stone - that panacea that would cure all sickness, including old age and death. Most of those scientists believed the sun orbited the earth." He paused, looked at me and asked "What assurance do you have that, in another hundred years, we won't look back at today's scientific pronouncements and giggle at the stupidity?"

Inadvertently I picked up my Scotch and stream water and drank from it. Then I recognized my error. Peabody saw my look of horror. "Don't worry Counselor," he reassured. "Single malt Scotch whisky will not only remove the disagreeable taste from water. It will also kill all bacteria, fungi and germs that might be present." With that guarantee, I took another drink and the Major continued to present his thesis.

"To justify federal government funded studies, college professors produce treatises claiming the universe will be sucked into a black hole in a billion years. Inexplicably, people with a life expectancy of only 83 years become terribly disturbed by the report. Some of the experts foresee collision with an asteroid while others claim San Francisco will slide into the Pacific. Still others threaten us with the probability of a volcanic eruption in Wyoming destroying all life on earth - with the possible exception of the cockroach.

"There are those nuts who, abetted by the news media's desperate attempts to increase viewer or readership count, feel they must periodically frighten the living bejaysus out of the simple minded." Peabody shook his head and mumbled, "Killer Bees from Brazil, Horse Encephalitis, Asian Bird Flu.

"Can you remember whatever highly publicized and

unavoidable cataclysm frightened you last year? - Or last month? - Or yesterday? Have the last few years' forecasts of increased hurricane activity come to pass? Has the construction of the Alaska pipeline destroyed the Elk migration patterns and led to the extinction of the species?

"If you take the alarmists seriously, you'll spend your lifetime scared to death by whatever disaster-of-the-month fright is popular. You'll be surrounded by more pills than are in a Wal-Mart pharmacy. Remember, this, young man. The quality of the ride is more important that the length of it. Life should be enjoyed, not spent cowering before an unbroken succession of largely imaginary fears."

As he turned to join his companions at the camp fire, he made one final comment. "If you paid less attention to global warming and more attention to the grill, perhaps the steaks you are supervising would not be cooked beyond the medium stage."

The Grasshopper and the Squirrel

Major Nathaniel Peabody stared out the kitchen window of his Philadelphia apartment. Even a casual observer would notice the lack of any sign of his usual buoyant disposition. He was concerned. His expression and his body language confirmed it. A wallet, a few bills and some coins lay on the counter before him. He picked up the wallet and shook it, hoping to discover some loose change still hiding within it. There was none.

He looked down at the entire extent of his financial resources and slowly shook his head. It was the morning of the thirtieth day of January and he knew his Spendthrift Trust wouldn't help him until the first day of February. Moreover, the attorney charged with the responsibility of delivering that check was out of town. He was trying a case in Harrisburg and wouldn't return until late that evening. He could be conned into providing tomorrow night's dinner. Tonight's dinner was another matter.

It was going to be a difficult thirty-three hours and seventeen minutes - the time until the clock would strike midnight on the 31st of January. Major Peabody often claimed he never missed a meal. He did, however, admit to having postponed several of them. Today, he faced the prospect of another set of postponements. And it wasn't only a matter of a lack of ready cash.

Peabody's refrigerator was less than well stocked. It contained an opened can of coffee, a potato, an onion, a partial loaf of bread and a half filled, small jar of domestic caviar. The caviar had been opened in November. It was used for Thanksgiving Day party hors d'oeuvres. The bread was not quite that old, but it had developed a grey/green mould. He threw it away. After a closer inspection of the potato and the caviar, they both joined the bread in the trash can.

The Major's dry goods larder was in even worse condition. It brought Old Mother Hubbard's cupboard to mind. Condiments and a can of mushrooms kept it from being entirely bare. Like the grasshopper in the Aesop fable, Peabody (as usual) had made absolutely no provision for his easily foreseeable future needs.

Peabody again counted the money lying on the kitchen counter and again shook his head. He could afford a McDonald's hamburger and a side order of fries. He had two dinners, a breakfast and a lunch to go until the cavalry arrived with his February 1 remittance. He might be able to squeeze by, but "squeezing by" was a distasteful activity.

Peabody fully expected to be trapped and unfed in his apartment for another day and a half. Contemplating his wretched financial condition, he stared out of the kitchen window. The antics of a squirrel living in the apartment building's backyard oak tree caught his attention. He watched as it came down the tree trunk. It paused while looking around to make sure no wolves or raptors were lurking nearby. Satisfied it was safe from attack, it busied itself digging in the frozen turf, looking for acorns planted sometime during the previous autumn.

The Major watched the squirrel's search. It dug here and there without result. He remembered watching the same squirrel during the late summer and fall as it harvested acorns from its tree home and planted them all over the yard. "It worked so hard to lay in supplies to provide winter meals," the Major mused. "Now, when hunger strikes, it is faced with the problem of remembering where it buried its provisions."

After a few minutes, the squirrel gave up. It stopped looking for the acorns and ran up a pole capped by a small, flat platform. It was a bird feeding station and the squirrel often stole seed from it. Like the Major's refrigerator, the feeding station was barren. Nevertheless, the squirrel sat there, apparently contemplating its own miserable situation.

At first, Peabody decided the squirrel was a very smart rodent to, at least, attempt to provide a cache of food for use when things were tough. He castigated himself. "I could have regularly shoved a few dollars into a shoe or under the mattress or some other such place where it would be safe from the bankers. If I ever needed it, I could search my apartment and, unlike that squirrel, I'd be able to find where I hid my rainy day fund. Then I'd have the wherewithal to provide for my end-of month meals."

Another moment of thought, however, brought a disturbing question to him. If he set aside money to provide for his very often late-in-the-month poverty, from whence would such money come? To create that fund, Peabody would be forced to reduce (or, worse, eliminate) the purchase of some of his standard monthly necessities.

Yes, he could built up a reserve, but it meant he would not be able to buy things like that extra case of 20 ga. shells now resting in his closet - or that box of cigars (now nearly empty) laying on the end table next to his wingback chair - or that liter of The Macallan now standing all alone in its usual place beneath the kitchen sink (and, incidentally, in desperate need of replenishment). Peabody blanched at the thought of foregoing those purchases and immediately changed his opinion of the squirrel.

"A dumb animal, that's what it is," he said aloud. "It spends countless hours creating a food supply. He hides acorns for future use and then forgets where he puts them. It sits there on a barren bird feeder, probably realizing it would be much better off if it had eaten the acorns when it first found them.

"If that squirrel were magically changed into a human being, it would probably do something foolish like giving part of its Spendthrift Trust check to some banker or broker and then die with a big bank account. Think of all the shotgun shells, all the fine cigars and all the single malt Scotch it would have missed."

At that moment, the back door of one of the building's ground floor apartments opened. The sound startled the squirrel. It leaped from the feeder and scurried up the oak tree. The Major, from his kitchen window, and the squirrel, from the safety of its perch on a high branch, watched a lady come out of the building with a coffee can half full of sunflower seeds. She dumped them on the empty bird feeder and returned to her apartment. As soon a she disappeared, the squirrel descended and made straight for the seeds.

"Perhaps that squirrel is smarter than I thought," Peabody mused. "All it has to do is make its presence known and some human will appear with enough food to appease its pangs of hunger. The squirrel depends upon others to save it from starvation. It'll stay fat all winter." Another thought occurred to Peabody. For the first time, he smiled. He picked up the phone and punched in a number.

"Hello, Doc," he said. "It's a gloomy, cold and dismal time of year. I thought you might need some cheering up. I know I do. I'll bet George the Third is depressed. You can't take him to a game farm for a workout in this kind of weather." Peabody paused while Doc Carmichael gave a report on the dog's current unhappy mental attitude. Then the Major resumed his attack.

"I've been thinking about last fall," he said. "Those were

great days - chasing Ruffed Grouse in Pennsylvania and Maine. We went to Wisconsin, too, didn't we?" Carmichael took over the conversation for a few moments. Then it was the Major's turn. "Have you eaten all the grouse you put in your freezer?'

He paused for Carmichael's response and then continued. "Good, Doc. Good," he said. "I've got a great idea. Why don't you bring a few over here? I'll cook 'em up and we'll have a feast." Carmichael's answer to Peabody's proposal was affirmative and enthusiastic.

"And while you're at it," Peabody added, "bring some flour and whatever kind of wine you like - and a couple of potatoes - bakers." He answered Doc Carmichael's next question with: "No, Doc, no. I don't need mushrooms or Bay leaf, but I'm a bit short of the Macallan."

Peabody replaced the phone in its charger. He smiled. "The lawyer gets back late tonight. He'll provide tomorrow's dinner. Let's see. I've got coffee and enough money to buy a pound of hamburger a loaf of bread and an onion. That will take care of breakfast and. lunch."

Peabody nodded and thought: "You can learn a lot from a smart squirrel. Make your presence known and, properly handled, someone will bring you a good meal."

Finding the Boar's Nest

Major Nathaniel Peabody was not in his apartment. He hadn't been there for three days. I didn't know exactly where he was, but I suspected he was hunting somewhere. It was nearing the end of the month, so I knew I'd soon learn where he was camped. He'd make contact and tell me where I should deliver his Spendthrift remittance. I hoped it was someplace that didn't require a passport.

I waited in my office. I waited and waited. The intercom buzzed. I picked up the phone and heard: "I'm at the Boar's Nest. Bring Upmann and Macallan. Friday. Six. Evergreen (click)." Translated into English, Major Peabody told me he was at a hunting camp in Michigan's Upper Peninsula. He asked me to meet him at a roadside tavern (The Evergreen) at 6 p.m. on Friday and bring a supply of H. Upmann cigars and Macallan single malt Scotch."

I've been at the Boar's Nest. Twice. The first time, I rented a car in Iron River and followed the map drawn by the Major and tried to find the place. My success was limited due to the quality of the map and the myriad of logging roads looping and criss-crossing through the dark the frightening forest.

At one point during that first visit, after the sun had set, I could see Coleman lantern lights shining off in the distance. I knew I wouldn't be able to find a road leading to them so I abandoned the car and walked cross-country toward them, hoping (no - praying) it was the Boar's Nest. That decision led to an unfortunate encounter with a skunk.

The second visit was not without complications. The car rental people recognized me and remembered the problems they had in de-odorizing the vehicle. They refused to let me hire any of their cars, but were kind enough to direct me to the local taxi company.

When the driver got as far as the Evergreen Inn, he took one look at the rutted trail leading from the tavern to the Boar's Nest and would go no further.

I met a friendly "Yooper" in the Evergreen. He was acquainted with the Boar's Nest, and, after a few bottles of beer, agreed to take me to the camp. I won't forget that trip. It was crowded in the front seat of the man's well-used pick-up truck. It was crowded because, in addition to the two of us, it was occupied by the Yooper's large dog. I believe it was part Labrador Retriever and part Budweiser Clydesdale. The animal was overly friendly and convinced it was a lap dog. It had bad breath.

On this trip, I was no longer a greenhorn. I knew the origin of the word "Yooper" (i.e. a person from Michigan's Upper Peninsula - i.e. a person from the U P - i.e. a Yooper). I also knew enough not to stop at the car rental agency in Iron River. They hold a grudge. A taxi took me to the Evergreen Inn.

It was four in the afternoon and the place wasn't crowded. A lone customer sat on a stool at the other side of the bar. I decided against ordering a martini for fear of being identify as a "flatlander". (That's a Yooper word meaning: a peculiar citified stranger from Lower Michigan.) I ordered a beer, intending to nurse it until Major Peabody appeared and drove me safely though that rabbit warren maze of two rutted trails surrounding the Boar's Nest.

A few minutes later, a flame orange capped hunter entered the tavern. He looked at me and immediately yelled out a greeting. "Hi Stinky." It was Steve, one of the Major's Yooper pals. I met him on my first visit to the Boar's Nest. "Bring me a martini, Jake," he said to the bartender. "Give my buddy whatever he's drinking," and he sat beside me. "Get here OK?" he asked. "Any skunk trouble?' Then he chuckled.

"Is this the guy you told us about?" Jake asked as he poured out a martini. "Stirred, not shaken," he explained to Steve who nodded his approval and answered: "Yah, this is the guy."

Jake went to get me another beer, and yelled over his shoulder. "Don't bring him in here if he finds another skunk. Leave him out in your truck."

"Whaddaya mean, 'leave him out in my truck'? I wouldn't let him in my truck. I'd tie a rope on him and let him run along behind me."

Those pleasantries taken care of, I was introduced and described as "a lawyer from Philadelphia".

The bartended extended his hand and introduced himself. "I'm Jake Green. I own the place. If you see any ways it can be improved, don't tell me about it. I'll sell it to you and you can make any changes you like."

The Yooper on the other side of the bar took it all in and decided to join the conversation. "Jake. Whaddaya mean letting a lawyer in here? You'll give this dump a bad name."

"It can't get any worse," Jake admitted. "I let you and this bum in." I thought he might have been talking about me, but he waved his hand toward Steve. Then, in too loud a voice to be confidential, he said to me "Be a little careful with Steve. He's a sensitive type. The only job he can get is sports writing for the local paper. He doesn't want respectable people to know he's sunk so low, so keep it under your hat"

"Yah'" then unnamed Yooper agreed. "The only story he ever wrote worth reading was that one about you finding the skunk - and that was two years ago."

I protested. I told them I hadn't been looking for a skunk. I admitted being lost in the woods and I admitted it scared the hell out of me. Anything can happen to you when you're on some UP logging trail in the middle of the night. Mosquitoes can bite you. You might get malaria. Snakes can sneak up on you. A bear can kill you and eat you. You can step on a skunk.

The three Yoopers looked at each other. For a split second, I thought they smiled, but they all solemnly nodded in agreement. Somebody said it was my turn. (That means it is my turn to buy everyone a drink.) I did so and the third Yooper came around the bar and joined us. His name was Dudley - or Marvin - or something. All three men offered suggestions.

When driving down strange logging road, Steve told me, always take the right hand turns going in and the left hand turns going out. Dudley or Marvin said I should always take the left hand turns going in and the right hand turns going out. As a heated argument ensued, I expected a fist fight, but the contenders calmed down when Jake said it was his turn.

Dudley or Marvin told me he used to get lost a lot back in the days when he had a Tates Compass. It always pointed to the southeast. After he threw it away and bought one that pointed to the north, he never again got lost. He advised me never to buy a Tates. (The Tates Compass Company motto is; He who has a Tates is lost. That doesn't seem to be a good company motto.)

Everyone agreed there are a lot trees between cars on Upper Michigan logging trails. Jake once got stuck and didn't have a "come-along" or even an ax to help get unstuck. He waited some time before he remembered how to get help. When he explained it, both Steve and Dudley or Marvin, corroborated the method and recommended it to me.

Whenever Jake finds himself in that kind of trouble, he goes to the side of the road and begins to relieve himself. He tells me nearly every time he does it, a car containing a bunch of women drives past. Then he said it was my turn again.

* * * * *

By the time Major Peabody arrived at the Evergreen Inn, it was after ten o'clock. He came in search of me because he and his friends at the Boar's Nest thought Steve must have driven into a ditch or got lost. (They'd sent him to pick me up.) The Major was surprised to find him with me and Jake and Dudley or Marvin. Peabody tells me we were standing in a circle and facing each other with arms interlaced as if we were imitating a 1930's football huddle. He says we were singing.

I don't remember any of it.

The Lesser of Two Evils

Philadelphians who do not migrate south in the wintertime resign themselves to hunkering down and surviving in the wet, miserable, bone chilling cold assaulting the city when January and February arrive and make them pay for their decision to live there. I am not comfortable in any place where water freezes in the streets and, at the first opportunity, turn itself into slush. As the temperature drops, my distress increases.

The Philadelphia weather was not the only factor accounting for my foul mood. I waited at the Smythe, Hauser, Engels & Tauchen Law Offices, expecting a (collect) telephone call from Major Peabody demanding the delivery of his Spendthrift Trust remittance.

Peabody enjoys torturing me by insisting I deliver his end-of-month check to some terrible, frightful location. I fully expected his phone call would come from north of the Arctic Circle where he would be hunting Musk Oxen or whatever he and his shot gunning friends hunt in some treeless, freezing place. It would probably be where the northern sun stays below the horizon and the mercury disappears into the thermometer's bulb.

It was, therefore, a pleasant surprise when he informed me he was in a camp in the warm desert outside of Gila Bend, Arizona, patiently awaiting delivery of his check. He told me I should bring four bags of ice cubes and a box of Dominican Republic cigars. He also told me the hunting season was in full swing and the California Quail were plentiful.

In a nanosecond, my world was bright and filled with

promise. The prospect of basking in the Arizona sun immediately destroyed my dark mood. When Charlotte made my flight reservation, she multiplied my cheerful spirits by adding an additional three days to the usual two day trip, pointing out the need for additional time because I might need a few extra days to find Major Peabody in the trackless desert.

Charlotte is a smart secretary. By giving me additional time in sunny Arizona, she insured herself of a great year-end performance review and the concomitant increase in salary. At the same time, she got rid of me for a week. As I said, I had been in a particularly nasty mood.

An early morning flight brought me to Phoenix. I hired a four-wheel drive vehicle and drove to Gila Bend. Following Peabody's directions, an hour later I found a camp consisting of a mobile trailer home, a tiny pop-up tent and a kind of portable gazebo - four aluminum poles stuck into the ground with netting around the sides and topped by a blue plastic roof.

The gazebo contained two large ice chests and two tables. One of them supported a number of plastic cups and a number of differently labeled bottles. The other was surrounded by fold-up chairs. Major Peabody sat in one of them. As I entered the gazebo, he asked if I brought the cigars. I handed the box to him. Then he asked if I brought the ice. I went to the Bronco, returned with the bags of ice cube and emptied them into the Styrofoam chests. Then he inquired into my health and well being.

My immediate chores completed. I sat in the gazebo, smiled, exhaled and enjoyed the Arizona desert. What wonderfully austere scenery. What a quiet and peaceful place. How nice and warm.

Wordlessly, the Major offer me a cigar. He knows I don't smoke. I declined and he unwrapped it and lit it up. For a time, not a word was spoken. I was almost reluctant to break the silence when I announced my intention to spend the rest of the week in the Major's company, enjoyed the perfect climate of the Sonoran desert.

Peabody seemed to stiffen. I thought I recognized an anxious look cross his face - an expression of surprise, of apprehension, of angst, perhaps of fear. It must have been my imagination. It was gone in an instant.

"I'm sure you'll enjoy your vacation from Philadelphia," he said, rather flatly. Somehow, the tone of his voice left me with the fleeting impression he was not enthusiastic about my decision to spend the days with him here, surrounded by the beautiful desert scenes. Of course, it occurred to me I might be imposing on him and his fellow hunters.

"Perhaps there's not enough room for me," I ventured.

"Not at all. Not at all," Peabody immediately answered. "There's no room in the trailer, but we can shuffle the supplies and gear around in that pop-up. I think we might make a cozy nest for you."

"I can sleep in the Bronco," I offered. "I can crack open the window and use the back seat. It's a bit cramped, but I can get along." The thought of spending four days coiled up in the back seat of the Bronco was not one calculated to fill me with joy. You have no idea of how much I hoped Peabody would argue with me. He did, thereby proving there is, in fact, a Supreme Being.

"No you can't sleep in that Bronco," Peabody argued. "You'd be too uncomfortable. You'd never get a good night's sleep. Besides, I don't think that car has been scorpion or tarantula proofed. Vehicles get hot in the daytime sun. At night when it gets cooler, scorpions and tarantulas like to crawl, inside warmer places. No, it would be better if you zipped up the pop-up and slept there.

Scorpions? Tarantulas? Great Scott!! My fear of scorpions

and tarantulas was exceeded only by my fear of rattlesnakes.

"I don't suppose there's enough room in the trailer? I could sleep on the floor or I could ..." Peabody interrupted me in mid-sentence.

"Counselor, if it were up to me ..." He paused and slowly shook his head. Then he explained. "It's Freddie's mobile trailer and he is a very particular cuss, He will allow only four people to stay in it. He wouldn't even let one of my Arizona friends join the hunt. That poor fellow is afraid of Gila monsters and rattlesnakes. He wanted to spend the nights inside the trailer, but Freddie was adamant. 'Four and no more' he insisted. Freddie's funny that way."

Gila monsters? Rattlesnakes? My God, what am I doing here?

"I'm afraid you'll have to sleep in the pop-up," Peabody concluded. "With a few blankets, you'll be warm and cozy." Peabody paused for a moment before adding: "Make sure you shake out the blankets before you get into bed. It'll get rid of the insects - probably. And shake out your shoes before you put them on in the morning."

I spent the night squatting on top of the front seat of the rented Bronco. I nearly went to sleep once. I was saved from that danger by a pack of wild coyotes. Their frightful howling shocked me into full consciousness. Their yelping was followed by silence and I am convinced the bloodthirsty beasts had surrounded my vehicle and lay there hoping I would emerge to relieve myself. I was ready to burst when the sun finally appeared.

I didn't wait for breakfast. I delivered the Major's remittance and immediately drove back to the Phoenix Sky Harbor Airport. Facing Philadelphia's snow and ice and sleet and soot, was, by far, the lesser of two evils.

The Peabody Proposal

When it comes to grouse hunting, those who are easily distracted seldom develop the degree of proficiency needed to qualify for the designation of "Expert". In fact, very few hunters can hope to attain even the "Gifted Amateur" title. Grouse hunting requires a single-minded concentration difficult to maintain, especially since the hunting season opens during the best time of the year.

As soon as the hunter begins to muse about the beautiful color in a stand of hard maple, or directs his attention to the beech log he must step over, you may be assured some nearby grouse will say "Let's see if he has a weak bladder," and explode out of the undergrowth causing the hunter to drop his shotgun and use language guaranteed to teach new words to any minister who may be picking black berries in the vicinity.

The incidence of bladder accident among duck hunters, on the other hand, is statistically insignificant. They usually see their quarry approaching from afar. If the duck hunter's attention wanders, a good retriever - with eyesight so superior to that of his master - will often twitch or raise his head or make some kind of movement to jolt the hunter from his reverie and put him on the alert.

Duck hunting does not demand constant vigilance. There are many periods of inactivity when the horizon is barren of birds, the coffee has been safely poured from the thermos, the decoy layout requires no fiddling and neither temperature nor wind velocity force the hunter to hunker down and limit his attentions to the damnedable snow or rain or wind (or combination thereof) which assail him.

Major Peabody had no cause for such complaint as he sat in his Boulder Lake shore blind. It was a bluebird morning. His hunting companion, Hans, was not in a talkative mood. Hans tends to be a taciturn type, but, then, generally speaking, Labrador Retrievers are not garrulous. Sitting alone, the Major was reduced to watching little black specks, probably Bluebill, congregating far out in the middle of the lake.

Canadian weather patterns had not yet produced enough cold air to cause large numbers of birds to start their southern migration along the Mississippi flyway. Peabody wondered if there were other reasons why he could find no flocks of ducks anywhere in the sky. Certainly, there weren't as many water-fowl as there were back in the 1950s when a much younger Nathaniel Peabody got his first 20 ga. single shot and began to hunt them.

After checking to make sure there were no ducks in the sky, the Major continued his musings. He approached the subject in his usual direct and logical manner. There were fewer ducks in the air because there were fewer ducks. There were fewer ducks because the hens were laying fewer eggs. The hens were laying fewer eggs because there were fewer wetland areas available for duck reproduction activities.

If you destroy all the bedrooms and all the backseats of automobiles in the world, the number of human beings will decrease. The conclusion was inescapable. No wetland habitat means no thriving duck population.

Peabody considered the work of the Ducks Unlimited organization and their labors to create and preserve wetlands for duck habitat. Great work, but not nearly enough. The growth of cities and urban and suburban developments undoubtedly contributed to the problem, but the main reason for the damage to the duck population was the drainage of wetlands in order to increase the amount of land needed for agricultural purposes.

Peabody remembered how the Roosevelt Administration approached a 1930s Depression problem. The farm economy was on the fritz. It cost the farmer more to grow his crops than the amount the market would pay for them The Federal government stepping in. It paid the farmer for plowing under every second row of corn and for killing every third pig.

It was an example of the successful application of basic supply side economics. Limit supply and demand will increase. Peabody reversed the proposition. If you decrease the demand, the supply will be increased. The logic is irrefutable. Peabody had found the answer to reconstituting the nation's waterfowl populations.

A Federal government program should be adopted immediately. The government should pay a bounty for the killing of every other person in the United States - citizen or illegal immigrant, it doesn't matter. A smaller supply of people means a smaller demand for food. A smaller demand for food means no need for the further drainage of wetlands. It also means land currently under cultivation, but no longer needed for food production, could go wild and return to being wetland and wild life habitat.

There would be more wetlands. There would be more ducks.

Such a government program would appeal to others in additional to duck hunters. Land used to produce corn will become fallow. The pheasant and Hungarian Partridge populations will increase. Upland game hunters will have to assume the heavy responsibility of keeping their number under control.

With only half the number of people available to eat meat

and drink milk, cattle herds can be reduced by fifty percent. That means the bossy cow production of methane gas will be cut in half and the quasi-environmentalists will, thus, be assured the world's atmosphere will be saved.

With half the automobile drivers exterminated, half the motor vehicles will sit unused and rusting in residential garages. The smog, the carbon monoxide and the sulfides they spew into the air will discontinue. Global warming will cease to be a problem and the quasi-environmentalists will have to abandon their cause and find productive work. There will be only half the number of drunken drivers aiming their cars at us and we'll have twice the amount of room to dodge them on the highways.

The program is not one without the dangers of unforeseen consequences. The citizenry might take it upon themselves to polish off all those who deserve it. More than half the population might be killed and, certainly, all of the politicians in the United States would be put at risk.

The plan will require the involvement of Congress. Senators and Representatives won't consider funding any program unless it creates a flourishing bureaucracy to regulate it. Moreover, government licensing, seasons and bag limits are necessary. Without carefully drawn regulations, Peabody thought, some fool might try to kill him.

At that moment, Hans opened his eyes, stiffened and raised his nose a few inches above the paws upon which it rested. He turned his head slightly to the left. The Major noticed the movement and carefully looked to the sky. He saw a flock of Bluebill descending in preparation for a swing over his decoys.

Peabody's project was immediately forgotten and received no further treatment.

Compromise

Major Nathaniel Peabody had worked himself into a corner. He was committed to travel to Uruguay to hunt Perdiz and Grey Winged Doves. He paid the airlines and the outfitter, but had nothing left to pay incidental expenses. He had been tenacious. I had been obstinate. "You lawyers have a bad reputation," he said, testily, after I refused his third or fourth request for an advance payment from the Peabody Spendthrift Trust.

"Largely undeserved," I countered, expecting the overwhelming logic of my simple statement would be enough to quiet him. Somehow it didn't work.

"Oh?" he answered. I didn't have to look at him. I knew he had raised his eyebrows, intending to indicate both surprise and disbelief. "Look at all the damage lawyers do to innocent people just because of some silly clause in a trust agreement," he fired back and quickly went on, before I could respond. "Most of the people in Congress are lawyers and just look at all the disasters they cause by the stupid laws they enact."

I protested. "A majority of the people in Congress may have law degrees," I admitted, "but that doesn't make them lawyers. Most of them have never practiced law for a day in their entire lives. They went from law school directly into politics. Oh, some of them might have been a Prosecuting Attorney for a few years and had some slight experience trying to jail people guilty of misdemeanors, but that isn't really practicing law."

"Nevertheless," Peabody insisted, "those Congress people

are lawyers and I am forced to agree with you. They are incompetent." Then, looking directly at me and, slowly, in a disparaging tone, he added: "There's no law requiring any lawyer to know what he's doing." He emphasized "any" and made me feel quite uncomfortable.

Peabody continued without pausing, giving me no opportunity to interrupt and correct his misquotes. "Once the people you characterize as incompetent lawyers get into Congress," he said, "they feel they must justify their existence by passing laws. They amend and patch and tinker with clearly written proposed legislation until it covers thousands of pages and is entirely incomprehensible.

"Of course, they do it on purpose. It is meant to provide income for their fellow attorneys. Think of the number of lawsuits started because a judge is required to try to make sense out of incomprehensible legislation. Every one of those cases represents an expense for the clients and a source of income for the lawyers." Peabody paused and lit a cigar.

Clearly, the Major intended to continue to attack attorneys in general and me in particular because of the requirement that I follow the terms of the Peabody Spendthrift Trust. It was time for me to mount my defense. "There is a germ of validity in your comment," I admitted, emphasizing the words 'a germ'. "However, you can't blame the legal profession. Remember, it is people like you who elect the incompetent members of Congress and people like you who keep them in office when they run for re-election."

I had the satisfaction of watching Peabody scowl and look like he just bit into a Florida Key lime. It showed he recognized the truth of my argument. I was on a roll and didn't want to give him an opportunity to recover. Before he could answer, I proceeded to distinguish my kind of law practice from the kinds he berated.

"Your germ of truth lies in the fact that poorly designed legislation gives rise to unintended consequences. And those unintended consequences give rise to lawsuits. Private practitioners, on the other hand, are particularly careful to prepare documents in unambiguous terms which require no judicial interpretations." Now I was ready to deliver the coup-de-grace.

"The Peabody Spendthrift Trust is an excellent example. It says: NO PREPAYMENTS. It cannot be misinterpreted. Its language is crystal clear. That's the kind of clarity in contract provisions that saves our clients from future expensive litigation.

"In those rare situations when a contract is not entirely clear," I added, "we protect our clients' interests as well as their pocket books by avoiding courtroom battles. We seldom adopt intransigent positions. That's the sort of thing that results in confrontation and expensive litigation. Litigation is more than expensive. It is risky. Lord only knows what a jury will do. Not even the Lord knows what a judge will do. We tend to be arbiters. Most civil law problems are not resolved in the courtroom. They are settled at the conference table. A good civil attorney is a genius at compromise."

"Really?" Peabody questioned. He thought for a while, blew a smoke ring and, surprised me by abruptly changing the subject. "For God's sakes, young man," he blurted out, "it's only a matter of eight days until the first of the month. Do you want me to arrive in Uruguay without a cent? If I'm careful, I could limit my shooting requirement to 4 cases of shells, but they cost ten dollars a box. Do you want me to stand there, aim my Lefever at a Perdiz and yell out "Bang, Bang?

"And there are the gratuities," he muttered. "A hundred and fifty for the guides and fifty for the lodge staff is the absolute minimum. Do you want me to look like a miserly tightwad?

Surely a respected, conscientious and crafty member of the bar - much like you - could find a way to save me from such a dishonorable predicament. To use the word you so eloquently used, can't we find some sort of..." Peabody paused before emphasizing the word... "compromise?"

Peabody was trying his best to peddle guilt. He was trying to shame me into allowing an advanced trust fund payment and I would have none of it. Yes, I opened the door to argument when I inadvertently mentioned the word 'compromise', but I was sure I could recover from that error. I meant to stick to my guns.

"Compromise," I explained to him, "does not mean 'surrender'. You would get a benefit if the unmistakably clear provisions of your Spendthrift Trust were modified, but the Trust itself would receive no balancing benefit. Without balancing equities, there can be no basis for compromise."

Peabody slowly nodded his head in agreement. He seemed resigned to start his Uruguayan hunt with little more than the change in his pockets. He sipped at the Macallan and again changed the subject.

"This will be an interesting trip," he said. "We'll leave Philadelphia in two days. A two-hour flight to Miami followed by a few hours layover and then an eleven-hour, late night flight over the Caribbean and South America will bring us to Buenos Aires. We'll land in the morning. After another layover, we'll fly to Montevideo and after still another layover, we'll get into some tiny puddle jumper airplane and continue on to Mercedes. From there it's only an hour by road to the estancia. I suspect the road may scream for surface attention."

"That journey sounds to me like a twenty hour ordeal," I said, trying to make pleasant conversation. "I'd be exhausted. I just can't sleep on an airplane. Regardless of the number of pillows they give me, I can never find a comfortable position."

Peabody leaned back in his chair. He looked at me and smiled. "I know," he said, "I know. I don't have the problem of sleeping on airplanes. I have a clear conscience. I can sleep anywhere." Peabody blew another smoke ring. He was smiling when he adding: "It is a shame you'll have to take that sleepless trip only because you must deliver a check to me on the first day of the month."

He waited a few moments while I considered the prospect of twenty hours cramped in an airplane seat and an hour of jolting over a seriously potholed road. Then the Major delivered his coup-de-grace. "It will be especially difficult for you," he said, "because we'll be returning on the afternoon of the same day you arrive at the estancia. You'll get there, delivery my check and then have to turn around and spend another twenty hours getting back to Philadelphia."

* * * * *

Luckily, I was able to negotiate a compromise. I delivered an early payment from the Peabody Spendthrift Trust and the Major promised to keep his mouth shut.

Is There Life Before Death

Whenever Major Peabody returns from one of his hunting forays, he calls from the Philadelphia airport. I drop everything, pick him up and drive him to his apartment. It's Standard Operating Procedure. That Standard Operating Procedure usually includes of a dinner and associated expenses (at my cost, of course).

The Major finished a five day turkey hunt in Texas. His flight was scheduled to arrive at 11 o'clock and I was ready to perform my post-hunt duties. But Peabody didn't call. The broken pattern bothered me. At one o'clock I called the airlines. The Major's flight arrived as per schedule.

The girl who answered the phone told me it was against company policy to divulge the name of any incoming passenger. I asked her if it was against company policy to divulge the name of anyone who was not on the passenger list. She laughed and told me she could do it. Then I asked if Nathaniel Peabody was not on the flight. She thought for as while and said. "No Nathaniel Peabody was not "not on the flight."

Peabody refused to immediately answer his phone. He let it ring and so did I. Finally, he picked it up. I was struck by the lackluster manner in which he spoke. He seemed preoccupied. His tone of voice as well as his failure to call from the airport were causes for concern. That concern was magnified when I made the usual invitation to dinner. He was reluctant to accept. After applying pressure and describing the quality of the ox joint and sauerkraut on the menu of his favorite German restaurant, he finally agreed.

Peabody's reactions were so un-Major-like, I knew something was up. I suspected it was serious. I cancelled my afternoon appointment and went to his apartment. I intended to find the reason for his extraordinary behavior. I pressed the buzzer on his door. The apartment was quiet. I pressed again and again. I heard him stir and the door opened.

"Oh, it's you. Hello Counselor." He stood in the doorway. His smile seemed a bit forced. "I'm afraid I won't be good company." He extended no invitation and made no movement suggesting I should enter and added: "Please don't misunderstand." It was Peabody's way of saying "Go away."

He began to close the door. I disregarded his unspoken order and walked past him into his living quarters. "Welcome back," I said. "Nice to see you." Peabody didn't answer. I took the glass from where it rested on the stand next to his wingback chair. The ice cubes had melted. It told me the Major had been sitting there for some time, thinking about something,

I went to the kitchen and prepared a drink. I gave it to him and went directly to the issue. "There are times when a man should not be alone. There are also times when he should talk about his problem with someone he can trust. That's what friends are for."

Peabody was silent. He sat, considered his lawyer's words and then spoke. "I'm not interested in encouraging your highly developed curiosity. At first, I was looking for a way to diplomatically tell you it was none of your business. Then it occurred to me. Perhaps you are right. The sooner I get this off my chest, the better I'll be." Then the Major told me about Peter Willson.

"I met Peter Willson in Texas. My first impression was decidedly negative. He had an unattractive imperious air about him. On the surface, he seemed aloof and cold, somewhat opinionated and conditioned to getting his own way. I suppose that's not uncommon among CEOs of large organizations. They are surrounded by sycophant underlings, ready to do their bidding and follow their orders while, all the time, currying their favor, stabbing their own competition in the back and waiting for the boss to retire or die.

"Peter sought me out and started questioning me about this and that. He was pushy and I don't like pushy people. However, he was a recent retiree and, I gave him a bit of leeway. After all, he spent nearly forty years in the corporate environment. That's enough to warp anyone.

"When I offered him a cigar, he told me he hadn't smoked in twenty years. Then he said 'My doctor can go to hell' and took it. I began to like him. I adjusted my first impression. It's possible he began to like me, too. In any even, he insisted on telling me his life story.

"Peter had rural beginnings. As a young man in Pennsylvania, he was a hunter and a fisher. He worked his way through the Wharton school and got a job in a bank. Once in the corporate world, his responsibilities began to grow. He could find no time for non-banking activities. Hunting and fishing disappeared from his life. I felt sorry for him.

"Of course, he became a workaholic. You don't crawl up the corporate ladder without being one. Peter became President of his bank. Then he arranged mergers with other groups and negotiated a few purchases, but never lost his position as top dog. He ended up as President of a large regional bank complex. As he approached retirement, his mind time-traveled back to earlier years. His youthful hunting and fishing experiences occupied more and more of his thoughts.

"Wilson retired three weeks ago. The Texas trek was his first hunt in decades. I suppose that's why he kept questioning me. He wanted to know what I could tell him about Ruffed Grouse hunting in Wisconsin, about pheasants in South Dakota, ducks in Nicaragua, Perdiz in Uruguay and quail in Georgia. It wasn't mere curiosity. He said he was retired - he was now a free man. He intended to go there and do it."

Peabody leaned back, sipped and continued his story. He wasn't talking to me. He was speaking to some unseen audience.

"Yesterday, Peter Willson didn't return to camp for lunch. We found him still seated at the base of a tree. His shotgun lay across his lap. The turkey call had fallen from his hand. He was dead. I suppose it was a heart attack. When I packed his shaving gear, I found pills - Lisinopril, Plavix, Metropolol, one of those vastatin drugs with a name sounding like a Central Asian Republic - the stuff doctors prescribe for high blood pressure and elevated cholesterol.

"Well, Peter won't need them now. He won't go to Nicaragua or South Dakota. He won't shoot Perdiz or see Iguacu."

Peabody was quiet. Then for the first time since he began the story, he looked at me and asked a question. "Is there life before death? If Peter Willson were alive, he might say 'No'."

* * * * *

After reading the Peter Willson obituary in the Inquirer, I looked out my office window at the Philadelphia skyline, and repeated the Major's question. Is there life before death?

Too many people spend their lives only thinking about things they want to do and want to see. Too many people get to the ends of their lives and find there are too many things they haven't done and too many things they haven't seen. I've never given much serious thought to what I really want to do or what

I really want to see. Major Peabody is way ahead of me. He knows what he wants. And he does it.

Then I knew at least one thing I wanted to do. I drew a check on the Peabody Spendthrift Trust Fund and delivered it the Major - two weeks in advance of its due date.

Other Books by Galen Winter

LEGENDARY NORTHWOODS ANIMALS

Quasi-Scientific Studies of the Invisible Moose, the Shovel Nosed Beaver, the Blunt Billed Rock Pecker and Other Fabled Creatures. Charles Darwin - Roll Over in Your Grave.

BACKLASH

A Compendium of Lore and Lies (Mostly Lies) Concerning Hunting Fishing and the Out-Of-Doors

BACKLASH II

Tales Told by Hunters Fishermen and Other Damned Liars

THE AEGIS CONSPIRACY

A Novel About Conspiracies Within Conspiracies Within the CIA

THE BEST OF THE MAJOR

A Compilation of Stories About a Bird Hunter, a Rascal and a User of Cigars and Single Malt Scotch Whiskey

THE CHRONICLES OF MAJOR PEABODY

The Questionable Adventures of a Wily Spendthrift, a Politically Incorrect Curmudgeon, an Unprincipled Wagerer and an Obsessive Bird Hunter